# The Fugitive by John Galsworthy

A Play in Four Acts

John Galsworthy first published in 1897 with a collection of short stories entitled "The Four Winds". For the next 7 years he published these and all works under his pen name John Sinjohn. It was only upon the death of his father and the publication of "The Island Pharisees" in 1904 that he published as John Galsworthy. His first play was The Silver Box, an immediate success when it debuted in 1906 and was followed by "The Man of Property" later that same year and was the first in the Forsyte trilogy. Whilst today he is far more well know as a Nobel Prize winning novelist then he was considered a playwright dealing with social issues and the class system. We publish here 'The Fugitive' a great example of both his writing and his demonstration of how the class system worked at the time. He was appointed to the Order of Merit in 1929, after earlier turning down a knighthood, and awarded the Nobel Prize in 1932 though he was too ill to attend. John Galsworthy died from a brain tumour at his London home, Grove Lodge, Hampstead on January 31st 1933. In accordance with his will he was cremated at Woking with his ashes then being scattered over the South Downs from an aeroplane.

## Index O Contents

## PERSONS OF THE PLAY

GEORGE DEDMOND, a civilian
CLARE, his wife
GENERAL SIR CHARLES DEDMOND, K.C.B., his father.
LADY DEDMOND, his mother
REGINALD HUNTINGDON, Clare's brother
EDWARD FULLARTON, her friend
DOROTHY FULLARTON, her friend
PAYNTER, a manservant
BURNEY, a maid
TWISDEN, a solicitor
HAYWOOD, a tobacconist
MALISE, a writer
MRS. MILER, his caretaker
THE PORTER at his lodgings
A BOY messenger
ARNAUD, a waiter at "The Gascony"
MR. VARLEY, manager of "The Gascony"

TWO LADIES WITH LARGE HATS, A LADY AND GENTLEMAN, A LANGUID LORD, HIS COMPANION, A YOUNG MAN, A BLOND GENTLEMAN, A DARK GENTLEMAN.

ACT I. George Dedmond's Flat. Evening.

ACT II. The rooms of Malise. Morning.

ACT III. SCENE I. The rooms of Malice. Late afternoon.

ACT III SCENE II    The rooms of Malise. Early Afternoon.

ACT IV. A small supper room at "The Gascony."

Between Acts I and II three nights elapse.

Between Acts II and Act III, Scene I, three months.

Between Act III, Scene I, and Act III, Scene II, three months.

Between Act III, Scene II, and Act IV, six months.

"With a hey-ho chivy Hark forrard, hark forrard, tantivy!"

## ACT I

The SCENE is the pretty drawing-room of a flat. There are two doors, one open into the hall, the other shut and curtained. Through a large bay window, the curtains of which are not yet drawn, the towers of Westminster can be seen darkening in a summer sunset; a grand piano stands across one corner. The man-servant PAYNTER, clean-shaven and discreet, is arranging two tables for Bridge. BURNEY, the maid, a girl with one of those flowery Botticellian faces only met with in England, comes in through the curtained door, which she leaves open, disclosing the glimpse of a white wall. PAYNTER looks up at her; she shakes her head, with an expression of concern.

PAYNTER. Where's she gone?

BURNEY. Just walks about, I fancy.

PAYNTER. She and the Governor don't hit it! One of these days she'll flit—you'll see. I like her—she's a lady; but these thoroughbred 'uns—it's their skin and their mouths. They'll go till they drop if they like the job, and if they don't, it's nothing but jib, jib, jib. How was it down there before she married him?

BURNEY. Oh! Quiet, of course.

PAYNTER. Country homes—I know 'em. What's her father, the old Rector, like?

BURNEY. Oh! very steady old man. The mother dead long before I took the place.

PAYNTER. Not a penny, I suppose?

BURNEY. [Shaking her head] No; and seven of them.

PAYNTER. [At sound of the hall door] The Governor!

BURNEY withdraws through the curtained door. GEORGE DEDMOND enters from the hall. He is in evening dress, opera hat, and overcoat; his face is broad, comely, glossily shaved, but with neat moustaches. His eyes, clear, small, and blue-grey, have little speculation. His hair is well brushed.

GEORGE. [Handing PAYNTER his coat and hat] Look here, Paynter! When I send up from the Club for my dress things, always put in a black waistcoat as well.

PAYNTER. I asked the mistress, sir.

GEORGE. In future—see?

PAYNTER. Yes, sir. [Signing towards the window] Shall I leave the sunset, sir?

But GEORGE has crossed to the curtained door; he opens it and says: "Clare!" Receiving no answer, he goes in. PAYNTER switches up the electric light. His face, turned towards the curtained door, is apprehensive.

GEORGE. [Re-entering] Where's Mrs. Dedmond?

PAYNTER. I hardly know, sir.

GEORGE. Dined in?

PAYNTER. She had a mere nothing at seven, sir.

GEORGE. Has she gone out, since?

PAYNTER. Yes, sir—that is, yes. The, er, mistress was not dressed at all. A little matter of fresh air, I think; sir.

GEORGE. What time did my mother say they'd be here for Bridge?

PAYNTER. Sir Charles and Lady Dedmond were coming at half-past nine; and Captain Huntingdon, too—Mr. and Mrs. Fullarton might be a bit late, sir.

GEORGE. It's that now. Your mistress said nothing?

PAYNTER. Not to me, sir.

GEORGE. Send Burney.

PAYNTER. Very good, sir. [He withdraws.]

GEORGE stares gloomily at the card tables. BURNEY comes in front the hall.

GEORGE. Did your mistress say anything before she went out?

BURNEY. Yes, sir.

GEORGE. Well?

BURNEY. I don't think she meant it, sir.

GEORGE. I don't want to know what you don't think, I want the fact.

BURNEY. Yes, sir. The mistress said: "I hope it'll be a pleasant evening, Burney!"

GEORGE. Oh!—Thanks.

BURNEY. I've put out the mistress's things, sir.

GEORGE. Ah!

BURNEY. Thank you, sir. [She withdraws.]

GEORGE. Damn!

He again goes to the curtained door, and passes through. PAYNTER, coming in from the hall, announces: "General Sir Charles and Lady Dedmond." SIR CHARLES is an upright, well-groomed, grey-moustached, red-faced man of sixty-seven, with a keen eye for molehills, and none at all for mountains. LADY DEDMOND has a firm, thin face, full of capability and decision, not without kindliness; and faintly weathered, as if she had faced many situations in many parts of the world. She is fifty five. PAYNTER withdraws.

SIR CHARLES. Hullo! Where are they? H'm!

As he speaks, GEORGE re-enters.

LADY DEDMOND. [Kissing her son] Well, George. Where's Clare?

GEORGE. Afraid she's late.

LADY DEDMOND. Are we early?

GEORGE. As a matter of fact, she's not in.

LADY DEDMOND. Oh?

SIR CHARLES. H'm! Not—not had a rumpus?

GEORGE. Not particularly. [With the first real sign of feeling] What I can't stand is being made a fool of before other people. Ordinary friction one can put up with. But that—

SIR CHARLES. Gone out on purpose? What!

LADY DEDMOND. What was the trouble?

GEORGE. I told her this morning you were coming in to Bridge. Appears she'd asked that fellow Malise, for music.

LADY DEDMOND. Without letting you know?

GEORGE. I believe she did tell me.

LADY DEDMOND. But surely—

GEORGE. I don't want to discuss it. There's never anything in particular. We're all anyhow, as you know.

LADY DEDMOND. I see. [She looks shrewdly at her son] My dear, I should be rather careful about him, I think.

SIR CHARLES. Who's that?

LADY DEDMOND. That Mr. Malise.

SIR CHARLES. Oh! That chap!

GEORGE. Clare isn't that sort.

LADY DEDMOND. I know. But she catches up notions very easily. I think it's a great pity you ever came across him.

SIR CHARLES. Where did you pick him up?

GEORGE. Italy, this Spring, some place or other where they couldn't speak English.

SIR CHARLES. Um! That's the worst of travellin'.

LADY DEDMOND. I think you ought to have dropped him. These literary people [Quietly] From exchanging ideas to something else, isn't very far, George.

SIR CHARLES. We'll make him play Bridge. Do him good, if he's that sort of fellow.

LADY DEDMOND. Is anyone else coming?

GEORGE. Reggie Huntingdon, and the Fullartons.

LADY DEDMOND. [Softly] You know, my dear boy, I've been meaning to speak to you for a long time. It is such a pity you and Clare—What is it?

GEORGE. God knows! I try, and I believe she does.

SIR CHARLES. It's distressin'—for us, you know, my dear fellow— distressin'.

LADY DEDMOND. I know it's been going on for a long time.

GEORGE. Oh! leave it alone, mother.

LADY DEDMOND. But, George, I'm afraid this man has brought it to a point—put ideas into her head.

GEORGE. You can't dislike him more than I do. But there's nothing one can object to.

LADY DEDMOND. Could Reggie Huntingdon do anything, now he's home? Brothers sometimes

GEORGE. I can't bear my affairs being messed about—

LADY DEDMOND. Well! it would be better for you and Clare to be supposed to be out together, than for her to be out alone. Go quietly into the dining-room and wait for her.

SIR CHARLES. Good! Leave your mother to make up something. She'll do it!

LADY DEDMOND. That may be he. Quick!

[A bell sounds.] GEORGE goes out into the hall, leaving the door open in his haste. LADY DEDMOND, following, calls "Paynter!" PAYNTER enters.

LADY DEDMOND. Don't say anything about your master and mistress being out. I'll explain.

PAYNTER. The master, my lady?

LADY DEDMOND. Yes, I know. But you needn't say so. Do you understand?

PAYNTER. [In polite dudgeon] Just so, my lady.

[He goes out.]

SIR CHARLES. By Jove! That fellow smells a rat!

LADY DEDMOND. Be careful, Charles!

SIR CHARLES. I should think so.

LADY DEDMOND. I shall simply say they're dining out, and that we're not to wait Bridge for them.

SIR CHARLES. [Listening] He's having a palaver with that man of George's.

PAYNTER, reappearing, announces: "Captain Huntingdon." SIR CHARLES and LADY DEDMOND turn to him with relief.

LADY DEDMOND. Ah! It's you, Reginald!

HUNTINGDON. [A tall, fair soldier, of thirty] How d'you do? How are you, sir? What's the matter with their man?

SHE CHARLES. What!

HUNTINGDON. I was going into the dining-room to get rid of my cigar; and he said: "Not in there, sir. The master's there, but my instructions are to the effect that he's not."

SHE CHARLES. I knew that fellow—

LADY DEDMOND. The fact is, Reginald, Clare's out, and George is waiting for her. It's so important people shouldn't—

HUNTINGDON. Rather!

They draw together, as people do, discussing the misfortunes of members of their families.

LADY DEDMOND. It's getting serious, Reginald. I don't know what's to become of them. You don't think the Rector—you don't think your father would speak to Clare?

HUNTINGDON. Afraid the Governor's hardly well enough. He takes anything of that sort to heart so, especially Clare.

SIR CHARLES. Can't you put in a word yourself?

HUNTINGDON. Don't know where the mischief lies.

SIR CHARLES. I'm sure George doesn't gallop her on the road. Very steady-goin' fellow, old George.

HUNTINGDON. Oh, yes; George is all right, sir.

LADY DEDMOND. They ought to have had children.

HUNTINGDON. Expect they're pretty glad now they haven't. I really don't know what to say, ma'am.

SIR CHARLES. Saving your presence, you know, Reginald, I've often noticed parsons' daughters grow up queer. Get too much morality and rice puddin'.

LADY DEDMOND. [With a clear look] Charles!

SIR CHARLES. What was she like when you were kids?

HUNTINGDON. Oh, all right. Could be rather a little devil, of course, when her monkey was up.

SIR CHARLES. I'm fond of her. Nothing she wants that she hasn't got, is there?

HUNTINGDON. Never heard her say so.

SIR CHARLES. [Dimly] I don't know whether old George is a bit too matter of fact for her. H'm?

[A short silence.]

LADY DEDMOND. There's a Mr. Malise coming here to-night. I forget if you know him.

HUNTINGDON. Yes. Rather a thorough-bred mongrel.

LADY DEDMOND. He's literary. [With hesitation] You, you don't think he puts, er, ideas into her head?

HUNTINGDON. I asked Greyman, the novelist, about him; seems he's a bit of an Ishmaelite, even among those fellows. Can't see Clare—

LADY DEDMOND. No. Only, the great thing is that she shouldn't be encouraged. Listen!—It is her-coming in. I can hear their voices. Gone to her room. What a blessing that man isn't here yet! [The door bell rings] Tt! There he is, I expect.

SIR CHARLES. What are we goin' to say?

HUNTINGDON. Say they're dining out, and we're not to wait Bridge for them.

SIR CHARLES. Good!

The door is opened, and PAYNTER announces "Mr. Kenneth Malise." MALISE enters. He is a tall man, about thirty-five, with a strongly marked, dark, irregular, ironic face, and eyes which seem to have needles in their pupils. His thick hair is rather untidy, and his dress clothes not too new.

LADY DEDMOND. How do you do? My son and daughter-in-law are so very sorry. They'll be here directly.

[MALISE bows with a queer, curly smile.]

SIR CHARLES. [Shaking hands] How d'you do, sir?

HUNTINGDON. We've met, I think.

He gives MALISE that peculiar smiling stare, which seems to warn the person bowed to of the sort of person he is. MALISE'S eyes sparkle.

LADY DEDMOND. Clare will be so grieved. One of those invitations

MALISE. On the spur of the moment.

SIR CHARLES. You play Bridge, sir?

MALISE. Afraid not!

SIR CHARLES. Don't mean that? Then we shall have to wait for 'em.

LADY DEDMOND. I forget, Mr. Malise—you write, don't you?

MALISE. Such is my weakness.

LADY DEDMOND. Delightful profession.

SIR CHARLES. Doesn't tie you! What!

MALISE. Only by the head.

SIR CHARLES. I'm always thinkin' of writin' my experiences.

MALISE. Indeed!

[There is the sound of a door banged.]

SIR CHARLES. [Hastily] You smoke, Mr. MALISE?

MALISE. Too much.

SIR CHARLES. Ah! Must smoke when you think a lot.

MALISE. Or think when you smoke a lot.

SIR CHARLES. [Genially] Don't know that I find that.

LADY DEDMOND. [With her clear look at him] Charles!

The door is opened. CLARE DEDMOND in a cream-coloured evening frock comes in from the hall, followed by GEORGE. She is rather pale, of middle height, with a beautiful figure, wavy brown hair, full, smiling lips, and large grey mesmeric eyes, one of those women all vibration, iced over with a trained stoicism of voice and manner.

LADY DEDMOND. Well, my dear!

SIR CHARLES. Ah! George. Good dinner?

GEORGE. [Giving his hand to MALISE] How are you? Clare! Mr. MALISE!

CLARE. [Smiling-in a clear voice with the faintest possible lisp] Yes, we met on the door-mat. [Pause.]

SIR CHARLES. Deuce you did! [An awkward pause.]

LADY DEDMOND. [Acidly] Mr. Malise doesn't play Bridge, it appears. Afraid we shall be rather in the way of music.

SIR CHARLES. What! Aren't we goin' to get a game? [PAYNTER has entered with a tray.]

GEORGE. Paynter! Take that table into the dining room.

PAYNTER. [Putting down the tray on a table behind the door] Yes, sir.

MALISE. Let me give you a hand.

PAYNTER and MALISE carry one of the Bridge tables out, GEORGE making a half-hearted attempt to relieve MALISE.

SIR CHARLES. Very fine sunset!

Quite softly CLARE begins to laugh. All look at her first with surprise, then with offence, then almost with horror. GEORGE is about to go up to her, but HUNTINGDON heads him off.

HUNTINGDON. Bring the tray along, old man.

GEORGE takes up the tray, stops to look at CLARE, then allows HUNTINGDON to shepherd him out.

LADY DEDMOND. [Without looking at CLARE] Well, if we're going to play, Charles? [She jerks his sleeve.]

SIR CHARLES. What? [He marches out.]

LADY DEDMOND. [Meeting MALISE in the doorway] Now you will be able to have your music.

[She follows the GENERAL out] [CLARE stands perfectly still, with her eyes closed.]

MALISE. Delicious!

CLARE. [In her level, clipped voice] Perfectly beastly of me! I'm so sorry. I simply can't help running amok to-night.

MALISE. Never apologize for being fey. It's much too rare.

CLARE. On the door-mat! And they'd whitewashed me so beautifully! Poor dears! I wonder if I ought [She looks towards the door.]

MALISE. Don't spoil it!

CLARE. I'd been walking up and down the Embankment for about three hours. One does get desperate sometimes.

MALISE. Thank God for that!

CLARE. Only makes it worse afterwards. It seems so frightful to them, too.

MALISE. [Softly and suddenly, but with a difficulty in finding the right words] Blessed be the respectable! May they dream of me! And blessed be all men of the world! May they perish of a surfeit of good form!

CLARE. I like that. Oh, won't there be a row! [With a faint movement of her shoulders] And the usual reconciliation.

MALISE. Mrs. Dedmond, there's a whole world outside yours. Why don't you spread your wings?

CLARE. My dear father's a saint, and he's getting old and frail; and I've got a sister engaged; and three little sisters to whom I'm supposed to set a good example. Then, I've no money, and I can't do anything for a living, except serve in a shop. I shouldn't be free, either; so what's the good? Besides, I oughtn't to have married if I wasn't going to be happy. You see, I'm not a bit misunderstood or ill-treated. It's only—

MALISE. Prison. Break out!

CLARE. [Turning to the window] Did you see the sunset? That white cloud trying to fly up?

[She holds up her bare arms, with a motion of flight.]

MALISE. [Admiring her] Ah-h-h! [Then, as she drops her arms suddenly] Play me something.

CLARE. [Going to the piano] I'm awfully grateful to you. You don't make me feel just an attractive female. I wanted somebody like that. [Letting her hands rest on the notes] All the same, I'm glad not to be ugly.

MALISE. Thank God for beauty!

PAYNTER. [Opening the door] Mr. and Mrs. Fullarton.

MALISE. Who are they?

CLARE. [Rising] She's my chief pal. He was in the Navy.

She goes forward. MRS. FULLERTON is a rather tall woman, with dark hair and a quick eye. He, one of those clean-shaven naval men of good presence who have retired from the sea, but not from their susceptibility.

MRS. FULLARTON. [Kissing CLARE, and taking in both MALISE and her husband's look at CLARE] We've only come for a minute.

CLARE. They're playing Bridge in the dining-room. Mr. Malise doesn't play. Mr. Malise—Mrs. Fullarton, Mr. Fullarton.

[They greet.]

FULLARTON. Most awfully jolly dress, Mrs. Dedmond.

MRS. FULLARTON. Yes, lovely, Clare. [FULLARTON abases eyes which mechanically readjust themselves] We can't stay for Bridge, my dear; I just wanted to see you a minute, that's all. [Seeing HUNTINGDON coming in she speaks in a low voice to her husband] Edward, I want to speak to Clare. How d'you do, Captain Huntingdon?

MALISE. I'll say good-night.

He shakes hands with CLARE, bows to MRS. FULLARTON, and makes his way out. HUNTINGDON and FULLARTON foregather in the doorway.

MRS. FULLARTON. How are things, Clare? [CLARE just moves her shoulders] Have you done what I suggested? Your room?

CLARE. No.

MRS. FULLARTON. Why not?

CLARE. I don't want to torture him. If I strike—I'll go clean. I expect I shall strike.

MRS. FULLARTON. My dear! You'll have the whole world against you.

CLARE. Even you won't back me, Dolly?

MRS. FULLARTON. Of course I'll back you, all that's possible, but I can't invent things.

CLARE. You wouldn't let me come to you for a bit, till I could find my feet?

MRS. FULLARTON, taken aback, cannot refrain from her glance at FULLARTON automatically gazing at CLARE while he talks with HUNTINGDON.

MRS. FULLARTON. Of course—the only thing is that—

CLARE. [With a faint smile] It's all right, Dolly. I'm not coming.

MRS. FULLARTON. Oh! don't do anything desperate, Clare, you are so desperate sometimes. You ought to make terms, not tracks.

CLARE. Haggle? [She shakes her head] What have I got to make terms with? What he still wants is just what I hate giving.

MRS. FULLARTON. But, Clare—

CLARE. No, Dolly; even you don't understand. All day and every day —just as far apart as we can be—and still—Jolly, isn't it? If you've got a soul at all.

MRS. FULLARTON. It's awful, really.

CLARE. I suppose there are lots of women who feel as I do, and go on with it; only, you see, I happen to have something in me that comes to an end. Can't endure beyond a certain time, ever.

She has taken a flower from her dress, and suddenly tears it to bits. It is the only sign of emotion she has given.

MRS. FULLARTON. [Watching] Look here, my child; this won't do. You must get a rest. Can't Reggie take you with him to India for a bit?

CLARE. [Shaking her head] Reggie lives on his pay.

MRS. FULLARTON. [With one of her quick looks] That was Mr. Malise, then?

FULLARTON. [Coming towards them] I say, Mrs. Dedmond, you wouldn't sing me that little song you sang the other night, [He hums] "If I might be the falling bee and kiss thee all the day"? Remember?

MRS. FULLARTON. "The falling dew," Edward. We simply must go, Clare. Good-night. [She kisses her.]

FULLARTON. [Taking half-cover between his wife and CLARE] It suits you down to the ground-that dress.

CLARE. Good-night.

HUNTINGDON sees them out. Left alone CLARE clenches her hands, moves swiftly across to the window, and stands looking out.

HUNTINGDON. [Returning] Look here, Clare!

CLARE. Well, Reggie?

HUNTINGDON. This is working up for a mess, old girl. You can't do this kind of thing with impunity. No man'll put up with it. If you've got anything against George, better tell me. [CLARE shakes her head] You ought to know I should stick by you. What is it? Come?

CLARE. Get married, and find out after a year that she's the wrong person; so wrong that you can't exchange a single real thought; that your blood runs cold when she kisses you—then you'll know.

HUNTINGDON. My dear old girl, I don't want to be a brute; but it's a bit difficult to believe in that, except in novels.

CLARE. Yes, incredible, when you haven't tried.

HUNTINGDON. I mean, you—you chose him yourself. No one forced you to marry him.

CLARE. It does seem monstrous, doesn't it?

HUNTINGDON. My dear child, do give us a reason.

CLARE. Look! [She points out at the night and the darkening towers] If George saw that for the first time he'd just say, "Ah, Westminster! Clock Tower! Can you see the time by it?" As if one cared where or what it was—beautiful like that! Apply that to every —every—everything.

HUNTINGDON. [Staring] George may be a bit prosaic. But, my dear old girl, if that's all—

CLARE. It's not all—it's nothing. I can't explain, Reggie—it's not reason, at all; it's—it's like being underground in a damp cell; it's like knowing you'll never get out. Nothing coming, never anything coming again-never anything.

HUNTINGDON. [Moved and puzzled] My dear old thing; you mustn't get into fantods like this. If it's like that, don't think about it.

CLARE. When every day and every night! Oh! I know it's my fault for having married him, but that doesn't help.

HUNTINGDON. Look here! It's not as if George wasn't quite a decent chap. And it's no use blinking things; you are absolutely dependent on him. At home they've got every bit as much as they can do to keep going.

CLARE. I know.

HUNTINGDON. And you've got to think of the girls. Any trouble would be very beastly for them. And the poor old Governor would feel it awfully.

CLARE. If I didn't know all that, Reggie, I should have gone home long ago.

HUNTINGDON. Well, what's to be done? If my pay would run to it but it simply won't.

CLARE. Thanks, old boy, of course not.

HUNTINGDON. Can't you try to see George's side of it a bit?

CLARE. I do. Oh! don't let's talk about it.

HUNTINGDON. Well, my child, there's just one thing you won't go sailing near the wind, will you? I mean, there are fellows always on the lookout.

CLARE. "That chap, Malise, you'd better avoid him!" Why?

HUNTINGDON. Well! I don't know him. He may be all right, but he's not our sort. And you're too pretty to go on the tack of the New Woman and that kind of thing—haven't been brought up to it.

CLARE. British home-made summer goods, light and attractive—don't wear long. [At the sound of voices in the hall] They seem 'to be going, Reggie.

[HUNTINGDON looks at her, vexed, unhappy.]

HUNTINGDON. Don't head for trouble, old girl. Take a pull. Bless you! Good-night.

CLARE kisses him, and when he has gone turns away from the door, holding herself in, refusing to give rein to some outburst of emotion. Suddenly she sits down at the untouched Bridge table, leaning her bare elbows on it and her chin on her hands, quite calm. GEORGE is coming in. PAYNTER follows him.

CLARE. Nothing more wanted, thank you, Paynter. You can go home, and the maids can go to bed.

PAYNTER. We are much obliged, ma'am.

CLARE. I ran over a dog, and had to get it seen to.

PAYNTER. Naturally, ma'am!

CLARE. Good-night.

PAYNTER. I couldn't get you a little anything, ma'am?

CLARE. No, thank you.

PAYNTER. No, ma'am. Good-night, ma'am.

[He withdraws.]

GEORGE. You needn't have gone out of your way to tell a lie that wouldn't deceive a guinea-pig. [Going up to her] Pleased with yourself to-night? [CLARE shakes her head] Before that fellow MALISE; as if our own people weren't enough!

CLARE. Is it worthwhile to rag me? I know I've behaved badly, but I couldn't help it, really!

GEORGE. Couldn't help behaving like a shop-girl? My God! You were brought up as well as I was.

CLARE. Alas!

GEORGE. To let everybody see that we don't get on, there's only one word for it—Disgusting!

CLARE. I know.

GEORGE. Then why do you do it? I've always kept my end up. Why in heaven's name do you behave in this crazy way?

CLARE. I'm sorry.

GEORGE. [With intense feeling] You like making a fool of me!

CLARE. No—Really! Only, I must break out sometimes.

GEORGE. There are things one does not do.

CLARE. I came in because I was sorry.

GEORGE. And at once began to do it again! It seems to me you delight in rows.

CLARE. You'd miss your—reconciliations.

GEORGE. For God's sake, Clare, drop cynicism!

CLARE. And truth?

GEORGE. You are my wife, I suppose.

CLARE. And they twain shall be one—spirit.

GEORGE. Don't talk wild nonsense!

[There is silence.]

CLARE. [Softly] I don't give satisfaction. Please give me notice!

GEORGE. Pish!

CLARE. Five years, and four of them like this! I'm sure we've served our time. Don't you really think we might get on better together—if I went away?

GEORGE. I've told you I won't stand a separation for no real reason, and have your name bandied about all over London. I have some primitive sense of honour.

CLARE. You mean your name, don't you?

GEORGE. Look here. Did that fellow Malise put all this into your head?

CLARE. No; my own evil nature.

GEORGE. I wish the deuce we'd never met him. Comes of picking up people you know nothing of. I distrust him, and his looks, and his infernal satiric way. He can't even 'dress decently. He's not—good form.

CLARE. [With a touch of rapture] Ah-h!

GEORGE. Why do you let him come? What d'you find interesting in him?

CLARE. A mind.

GEORGE. Deuced funny one! To have a mind, as you call it, it's not necessary to talk about Art and Literature.

CLARE. We don't.

GEORGE. Then what do you talk about—your minds? [CLARE looks at him] Will you answer a straight question? Is he falling in love with you?

CLARE. You had better ask him.

GEORGE. I tell you plainly, as a man of the world, I don't believe in the guide, philosopher and friend business.

CLARE. Thank you.

A silence. CLARE suddenly clasps her hands behind her head.

CLARE. Let me go! You'd be much happier with any other woman.

GEORGE. Clare!

CLARE. I believe, I'm sure I could earn my living. Quite serious.

GEORGE. Are you mad?

CLARE. It has been done.

GEORGE. It will never be done by you, understand that!

CLARE. It really is time we parted. I'd go clean out of your life. I don't want your support unless I'm giving you something for your money.

GEORGE. Once for all, I don't mean to allow you to make fools of us both.

CLARE. But if we are already! Look at us. We go on, and on. We're a spectacle!

GEORGE. That's not my opinion; nor the opinion of anyone, so long as you behave yourself.

CLARE. That is behave as you think right.

GEORGE. Clare, you're pretty riling.

CLARE. I don't want to be horrid. But I am in earnest this time.

GEORGE. So am I.

[CLARE turns to the curtained door.]

GEORGE. Look here! I'm sorry. God knows I don't want to be a brute. I know you're not happy.

CLARE. And you—are you happy?

GEORGE. I don't say I am. But why can't we be?

CLARE. I see no reason, except that you are you, and I am I.

GEORGE. We can try.

CLARE. I HAVE—haven't you?

GEORGE. We used—

CLARE. I wonder!

GEORGE. You know we did.

CLARE. Too long ago—if ever.

GEORGE [Coming closer] I still—

CLARE. [Making a barrier of her hand] You know that's only cupboard love.

GEORGE. We've got to face the facts.

CLARE. I thought I was.

GEORGE. The facts are that we're married—for better or worse, and certain things are expected of us. It's suicide for you, and folly for me, in my position, to ignore that. You have all you can reasonably want; and I don't—don't wish for any change. If you could bring anything against me—if I drank, or knocked about town, or expected too much of you. I'm not unreasonable in any way, that I can see.

CLARE. Well, I think we've talked enough.

[She again moves towards the curtained door.]

GEORGE. Look here, Clare; you don't mean you're expecting me to put up with the position of a man who's neither married nor unmarried? That's simple purgatory. You ought to know.

CLARE. Yes. I haven't yet, have I?

GEORGE. Don't go like that! Do you suppose we're the only couple who've found things aren't what they thought, and have to put up with each other and make the best of it.

CLARE. Not by thousands.

GEORGE. Well, why do you imagine they do it?

CLARE. I don't know.

GEORGE. From a common sense of decency.

CLARE. Very!

GEORGE. By Jove! You can be the most maddening thing in all the world! [Taking up a pack of cards, he lets them fall with a long slithering flutter] After behaving as you have this evening, you might try to make some amends, I should think.

CLARE moves her head from side to side, as if in sight of something she could not avoid. He puts his hand on her arm.

CLARE. No, no—no!

GEORGE. [Dropping his hand] Can't you make it up?

CLARE. I don't feel very Christian.

She opens the door, passes through, and closes it behind her. GEORGE steps quickly towards it, stops, and turns back into the room. He goes to the window and stands looking out; shuts it with a bang, and again contemplates the door. Moving forward, he rests his hand on the deserted card table, clutching its edge, and muttering. Then he crosses to the door into the hall and switches off the light. He opens the door to go out, then stands again irresolute in the darkness and heaves a heavy sigh. Suddenly he mutters: "No!" Crosses resolutely back to the curtained door, and opens it. In the gleam of light CLARE is standing, unhooking a necklet. He goes in, shutting the door behind him with a thud.

CURTAIN.


## ACT II

The scene is a large, whitewashed, disordered room, whose outer door opens on to a corridor and stairway. Doors on either side lead to other rooms. On the walls are unframed reproductions of fine pictures, secured with tintacks. An old wine-coloured armchair of low and comfortable appearance, near the centre of the room, is surrounded by a litter of manuscripts, books, ink, pens and newspapers, as though someone had already been up to his neck in labour, though by a grandfather's clock it is only eleven. On a smallish table close by, are sheets of paper, cigarette ends, and two claret bottles. There are many books on shelves, and on the floor, an overflowing pile, whereon rests a soft hat, and a black knobby stick. MALISE sits in his armchair, garbed in trousers, dressing-gown, and slippers, unshaved and uncollared, writing. He pauses, smiles, lights a cigarette, and tries the rhythm of the last sentence, holding up a sheet of quarto MS.

MALISE. "Not a word, not a whisper of Liberty from all those excellent frock-coated gentlemen—not a sign, not a grimace. Only the monumental silence of their profound deference before triumphant Tyranny."

While he speaks, a substantial woman, a little over middle-age, in old dark clothes and a black straw hat, enters from the corridor. She goes to a cupboard, brings out from it an apron and a Bissell broom. Her movements are slow and imperturbable, as if she had much time before her. Her face is broad and dark, with Chinese eyebrows.

MALISE. Wait, Mrs. Miller!

MRS. MILER. I'm gettin' be'ind' and, sir.

She comes and stands before him. MALISE writes.

MRS. MILER. There's a man 'angin' about below.

MALISE looks up; seeing that she has roused his attention, she stops. But as soon as he is about to write again, goes on.

MRS. MILER. I see him first yesterday afternoon. I'd just been out to get meself a pennyworth o' soda, an' as I come in I passed 'im on the second floor, lookin' at me with an air of suspicion. I thought to meself at the time, I thought: You're a'andy sort of 'ang-dog man.

MALISE. Well?

MRS. MILER. Well-peekin' down through the balusters, I see 'im lookin' at a photograft. That's a funny place, I thinks, to look at pictures—it's so dark there, ye 'ave to use yer eyesight. So I giv' a scrape with me 'eel [She illustrates] an' he pops it in his pocket, and puts up 'is 'and to knock at number three. I goes down an' I says: "You know there's no one lives there, don't yer?" "Ah!" 'e says with an air of innercence, "I wants the name of Smithers." "Oh!" I says, "try round the corner, number ten." "Ah!" 'e says tactful, "much obliged." "Yes," I says, "you'll find 'im in at this time o' day. Good evenin'!" And I thinks to meself [She closes one eye] Rats! There's a good many corners hereabouts.

MALISE. [With detached appreciation] Very good, Mrs. Miler.

MRS. MILER. So this mornin', there e' was again on the first floor with 'is 'and raised, pretendin' to knock at number two. "Oh! you're still lookin' for 'im?" I says, lettin' him see I was 'is grandmother. "Ah!" 'e says, affable, "you misdirected me; it's here I've got my business." "That's lucky," I says, "cos nobody lives there neither. Good mornin'!" And I come straight up. If you want to see 'im at work you've only to go downstairs, 'e'll be on the ground floor by now, pretendin' to knock at number one. Wonderful resource!

MALISE. What's he like, this gentleman?

MRS. MILER. Just like the men you see on the front page o' the daily papers. Nasty, smooth-lookin' feller, with one o' them billycock hats you can't abide.

MALISE. Isn't he a dun?

MRS. MILER. They don't be'ave like that; you ought to know, sir. He's after no good. [Then, after a little pause] Ain't he to be put a stop to? If I took me time I could get 'im, innercent-like, with a jug o' water.

[MALISE, smiling, shakes his head.]

MALISE. You can get on now; I'm going to shave.

He looks at the clock, and passes out into the inner room. MRS. MILER, gazes round her, pins up her skirt, sits down in the armchair, takes off her hat and puts it on the table, and slowly rolls up her sleeves; then with her hands on her knees she rests. There is a soft knock on the door. She gets up leisurely and moves flat-footed towards it. The door being opened CLARE is revealed.

CLARE. Is Mr. Malise in?

MRS. MILER. Yes. But 'e's dressin'.

CLARE. Oh.

MRS. MILER. Won't take 'im long. What name?

CLARE. Would you say—a lady.

MRS. MILER. It's against the rules. But if you'll sit down a moment I'll see what I can do. [She brings forward a chair and rubs it with her apron. Then goes to the door of the inner room and speaks through it] A lady to see you. [Returning she removes some cigarette ends] This is my hour. I shan't make much dust. [Noting CLARE's eyebrows raised at the debris round the armchair] I'm particular about not disturbin' things.

CLARE. I'm sure you are.

MRS. MILER. He likes 'is 'abits regular.

Making a perfunctory pass with the Bissell broom, she runs it to the cupboard, comes back to the table, takes up a bottle and holds it to the light; finding it empty, she turns it upside down and drops it into the wastepaper basket; then, holding up the other bottle, and finding it not empty, she corks it and drops it into the fold of her skirt.

MRS. MILER. He takes his claret fresh-opened, not like these 'ere bawgwars.

CLARE. [Rising] I think I'll come back later.

MRS. MILER. Mr. Malise is not in my confidence. We keep each other to ourselves. Perhaps you'd like to read the paper; he has it fresh every mornin', the Westminister.

She plucks that journal from out of the armchair and hands it to CLARE, who sits doom again unhappily to brood. MRS. MILER makes a pass or two with a very dirty duster, then stands still. No longer hearing sounds, CLARE looks up.

MRS. MILER. I wouldn't interrupt yer with my workin,' but 'e likes things clean. [At a sound from the inner room] That's 'im; 'e's cut 'isself! I'll just take 'im the tobaccer!

She lifts a green paper screw of tobacco from the debris round the armchair and taps on the door. It opens. CLARE moves restlessly across the room.

MRS. MILER. [Speaking into the room] The tobaccer. The lady's waitin'.

CLARE has stopped before a reproduction of Titian's picture "Sacred and Profane Love." MRS. MILER stands regarding her with a Chinese smile. MALISE enters, a thread of tobacco still hanging to his cheek.

MALISE. [Taking MRS. MILER's hat off the table and handing it to her] Do the other room.

[Enigmatically she goes.]

MALISE. Jolly of you to come. Can I do anything?

CLARE. I want advice-badly.

MALISE. What! Spreading your wings?

CLARE. Yes.

MALISE. Ah! Proud to have given you that advice. When?

CLARE. The morning after you gave it me...

MALISE. Well?

CLARE. I went down to my people. I knew it would hurt my Dad frightfully, but somehow I thought I could make him see. No good. He was awfully sweet, only—he couldn't.

MALISE. [Softly] We English love liberty in those who don't belong to us. Yes.

CLARE. It was horrible. There were the children—and my old nurse. I could never live at home now. They'd think I was—. Impossible —utterly! I'd made up my mind to go back to my owner—And then— he came down himself. I couldn't d it. To be hauled back and begin all over again; I simply couldn't. I watched for a chance; and ran to the station, and came up to an hotel.

MALISE. Bravo!

CLARE. I don't know, no pluck this morning! You see, I've got to earn my living—no money; only a few things I can sell. All yesterday I was walking about, looking at the women. How does anyone ever get a chance?

MALISE. Sooner than you should hurt his dignity by working, your husband would pension you off.

CLARE. If I don't go back to him I couldn't take it.

MALISE. Good!

CLARE. I've thought of nursing, but it's a long training, and I do so hate watching pain. The fact is, I'm pretty hopeless; can't even do art work. I came to ask you about the stage.

MALISE. Have you ever acted? [CLARE shakes her head] You mightn't think so, but I've heard there's a prejudice in favour of training. There's Chorus—I don't recommend it. How about your brother?

CLARE. My brother's got nothing to spare, and he wants to get married; and he's going back to India in September. The only friend I should care to bother is Mrs. Fullarton, and she's got a husband.

MALISE. I remember the gentleman.

CLARE. Besides, I should be besieged day and night to go back. I must lie doggo somehow.

MALISE. It makes my blood boil to think of women like you. God help all ladies without money.

CLARE. I expect I shall have to go back.

MALISE. No, no! We shall find something. Keep your soul alive at all costs. What! let him hang on to you till you're nothing but emptiness and ache, till you lose even the power to ache. Sit in his drawing-room, pay calls, play Bridge, go out with him to dinners, return to—duty; and feel less and less, and be less and less, and so grow old and die!

[The bell rings.]

MALISE. [Looking at the door in doubt] By the wayhe'd no means of tracing you?

[She shakes her head.] [The bell rings again.]

MALISE. Was there a man on the stairs as you came up?

CLARE. Yes. Why?

MALISE. He's begun to haunt them, I'm told.

CLARE. Oh! But that would mean they thought I—oh! no!

MALISE. Confidence in me is not excessive.

CLARE. Spying!

MALISE. Will you go in there for a minute? Or shall we let them ring or what? It may not be anything, of course.

CLARE. I'm not going to hide.

[The bell rings a third time.]

MALISE. [Opening the door of the inner room] Mrs. Miler, just see who it is; and then go, for the present.

MRS. MILER comes out with her hat on, passes enigmatically to the door, and opens it. A man's voice says: "Mr. Malise? Would you give him these cards?"

MRS. MILER. [Re-entering] The cards.

MALISE. Mr. Robert Twisden. Sir Charles and Lady Dedmond. [He looks at CLARE.]

CLARE. [Her face scornful and unmoved] Let them come.

MALISE. [TO MRS. MILER] Show them in!

TWISDEN enters-a clean-shaved, shrewd-looking man, with a fighting underlip, followed by SIR CHARLES and LADY DEDMOND. MRS. MILER goes. There are no greetings.

TWISDEN. Mr. Malise? How do you do, Mrs. Dedmond? Had the pleasure of meeting you at your wedding. [CLARE inclines her head] I am Mr. George Dedmond's solicitor, sir. I wonder if you would be so very kind as to let us have a few words with Mrs. Dedmond alone?

At a nod from CLARE, MALISE passes into the inner room, and shuts the door. A silence.

SIR CHARLES. [Suddenly] What!

LADY DEDMOND. Mr. Twisden, will you—?

TWISDEN. [Uneasy] Mrs. Dedmond I must apologize, but you—you hardly gave us an alternative, did you? [He pauses for an answer, and, not getting one, goes on] Your disappearance has given your husband great anxiety. Really, my dear madam, you must forgive us for this—attempt to get into communication.

CLARE. Why did you spy, HERE?

SIR CHARLES. No, no! Nobody's spied on you. What!

TWISDEN. I'm afraid the answer is that we appear to have been justified. [At the expression on CLARE'S face he goes on hastily] Now, Mrs. Dedmond, I'm a lawyer and I know that appearances are misleading. Don't think I'm unfriendly; I wish you well. [CLARE raises her eyes. Moved by that look, which is exactly as if she had said: "I have no friends," he hurries on] What we want to say to you is this: Don't let this split go on! Don't commit yourself to what you'll bitterly regret. Just tell us what's the matter. I'm sure it can be put straight.

CLARE. I have nothing against my husband, it was quite unreasonable to leave him.

TWISDEN. Come, that's good.

CLARE. Unfortunately, there's something stronger than reason.

TWISDEN. I don't know it, Mrs. Dedmond.

CLARE. No?

TWISDEN. [Disconcerted] Are you—you oughtn't to take a step without advice, in your position.

CLARE. Nor with it?

TWISDEN. [Approaching her] Come, now; isn't there anything you feel you'd like to say—that might help to put matters straight?

CLARE. I don't think so, thank you.

LADY DEDMOND. You must see, Clare, that—

TWISDEN. In your position, Mrs. Dedmond—a beautiful young woman without money. I'm quite blunt. This is a hard world. Should be awfully sorry if anything goes wrong.

CLARE. And if I go back?

TWISDEN. Of two evils, if it be so—choose the least!

CLARE. I am twenty-six; he is thirty-two. We can't reasonably expect to die for fifty years.

LADY DESMOND. That's morbid, Clare.

TWISDEN. What's open to you if you don't go back? Come, what's your position? Neither fish, flesh, nor fowl; fair game for everybody. Believe me, Mrs. Dedmond, for a pretty woman to strike, as it appears you're doing, simply because the spirit of her marriage has taken flight, is madness. You must know that no one pays attention to anything but facts. If now—excuse me—you—you had a lover, [His eyes travel round the room and again rest on her] you would, at all events, have some ground under your feet, some sort of protection, but [He pauses] as you have not—you've none.

CLARE. Except what I make myself.

SIR CHARLES. Good God!

TWISDEN. Yes! Mrs. Dedmond! There's the bedrock difficulty. As you haven't money, you should never have been pretty. You're up against the world, and you'll get no mercy from it. We lawyers see too much of that. I'm putting it brutally, as a man of the world.

CLARE. Thank you. Do you think you quite grasp the alternative?

TWISDEN. [Taken aback] But, my dear young lady, there are two sides to every contract. After all, your husband's fulfilled his.

CLARE. So have I up till now. I shan't ask anything from him, nothing, do you understand?

LADY DEDMOND. But, my dear, you must live.

TWISDEN. Have you ever done any sort of work?

CLARE. Not yet.

TWISDEN. Any conception of the competition nowadays?

CLARE. I can try.

[TWISDEN, looking at her, shrugs his shoulders]

CLARE. [Her composure a little broken by that look] It's real to me—this—you see!

SIR CHARLES. But, my dear girl, what the devil's to become of George?

CLARE. He can do what he likes—it's nothing to me.

TWISDEN. Mrs. Dedmond, I say without hesitation you've no notion of what you're faced with, brought up to a sheltered life as you've been. Do realize that you stand at the parting of the ways, and one leads into the wilderness.

CLARE. Which?

TWISDEN. [Glancing at the door through which MALISE has gone] Of course, if you want to play at wild asses there are plenty who will help you.

SIR CHARLES. By Gad! Yes!

CLARE. I only want to breathe.

TWISDEN. Mrs. Dedmond, go back! You can now. It will be too late soon. There are lots of wolves about. [Again he looks at the door]

CLARE. But not where you think. You say I need advice. I came here for it.

TWISDEN. [With a curiously expressive shrug] In that case I don't know that I can usefully stay.

[He goes to the outer door.]

CLARE. Please don't have me followed when I leave here. Please!

LADY DEDMOND. George is outside, Clare.

CLARE. I don't wish to see him. By what right have you come here? [She goes to the door through which MALISE has passed, opens it, and says] Please come in, Mr. Malise.

[MALISE enters.]

TWISDEN. I am sorry. [Glancing at MALISE, he inclines his head] I am sorry. Good morning. [He goes]

LADY DEDMOND. Mr. Malise, I'm sure, will see—

CLARE. Mr. Malise will stay here, please, in his own room.

[MALISE bows]

SIR CHARLES. My dear girl, 'pon my soul, you know, I can't grasp your line of thought at all!

CLARE. No?

LADY DEDMOND. George is most willing to take up things just as they were before you left.

CLARE. Ah!

LADY DEDMOND. Quite frankly—what is it you want?

CLARE. To be left alone. Quite frankly, he made a mistake to have me spied on.

LADY DEDMOND. But, my good girl, if you'd let us know where you were, like a reasonable being. You can't possibly be left to yourself without money or position of any kind. Heaven knows what you'd be driven to!

MALISE. [Softly] Delicious!

SIR CHARLES. You will be good enough to repeat that out loud, sir.

LADY DEDMOND. Charles! Clare, you must know this is all a fit of spleen; your duty and your interest—marriage is sacred, Clare.

CLARE. Marriage! My marriage has become the—the reconciliation—of two animals—one of them unwilling. That's all the sanctity there is about it.

SIR CHARLES. What!

[She looks at MALISE]

LADY DEDMOND. You ought to be horribly ashamed. CLARE. Of the fact-I am.

LADY DEDMOND. [Darting a glance at MALISE] If we are to talk this out, it must be in private.

MALISE. [To CLARE] Do you wish me to go?

CLARE. No.

LADY DEDMOND. [At MALISE] I should have thought ordinary decent feeling—Good heavens, girl! Can't you see that you're being played with?

CLARE. If you insinuate anything against Mr. Malise, you lie.

LADY DEDMOND. If you will do these things—come to a man's rooms—

CLARE. I came to Mr. Malise because he's the only person I know with imagination enough to see what my position is; I came to him a quarter of an hour ago, for the first time, for definite advice, and you instantly suspect him. That is disgusting.

LADY DEDMOND. [Frigidly] Is this the natural place for me to find my son's wife?

CLARE. His woman.

LADY DEDMOND. Will you listen to Reginald?

CLARE. I have.

LADY DEDMOND. Haven't you any religious sense at all, Clare?

CLARE. None, if it's religion to live as we do.

LADY DEDMOND. It's terrible—this state of mind! It's really terrible!

CLARE breaks into the soft laugh of the other evening. As if galvanized by the sound, SIR CHARLES comes to life out of the transfixed bewilderment with which he has been listening.

SIR CHARLES. For God's sake don't laugh like that!

[CLARE Stops]

LADY DEDMOND. [With real feeling] For the sake of the simple right, Clare!

CLARE. Right? Whatever else is right—our life is not. [She puts her hand on her heart] I swear before God that I've tried and tried. I swear before God, that if I believed we could ever again love each other only a little tiny bit, I'd go back. I swear before God that I don't want to hurt anybody.

LADY DEDMOND. But you are hurting everybody. Do, do be reasonable!

CLARE. [Losing control] Can't you see that I'm fighting for all my life to come—not to be buried alive—not to be slowly smothered. Look at me! I'm not wax—I'm flesh and blood. And you want to prison me forever—body and soul.

[They stare at her]

SIR CHARLES. [Suddenly] By Jove! I don't know, I don't know! What!

LADY DEDMOND. [To MALISE] If you have any decency left, sir, you will allow my son, at all events, to speak to his wife alone. [Beckoning to her husband] We'll wait below.

SIR CHARLES. I, I want to speak. [To CLARE] My dear, if you feel like this, I can only say as a, as a gentleman—

LADY DEDMOND. Charles!

SIR CHARLES. Let me alone! I can only say that—damme, I don't know that I can say anything!

He looks at her very grieved, then turns and marches out, followed by LADY DEDMOND, whose voice is heard without, answered by his: "What!" In the doorway, as they pass, GEORGE is standing; he comes in.

GEORGE. [Going up to CLARE, who has recovered all her self-control] Will you come outside and speak to me?

CLARE. No.

GEORGE glances at MALISE, who is leaning against the wall with folded arms.

GEORGE. [In a low voice] Clare!

CLARE. Well!

GEORGE. You try me pretty high, don't you, forcing me to come here, and speak before this fellow? Most men would think the worst, finding you like this.

CLARE. You need not have come—or thought at all.

GEORGE. Did you imagine I was going to let you vanish without an effort—

CLARE. To save me?

GEORGE. For God's sake be just! I've come here to say certain things. If you force me to say them before him—on your head be it! Will you appoint somewhere else?

CLARE. No.

GEORGE. Why not?

CLARE. I know all those "certain things." "You must come back. It is your duty. You have no money. Your friends won't help you. You can't earn your living. You are making a scandal." You might even say for the moment: "Your room shall be respected."

GEORGE. Well, it's true and you've no answer.

CLARE. Oh! [Suddenly] Our life's a lie. It's stupid; it's disgusting. I'm tired of it! Please leave me alone!

GEORGE. You rather miss the point, I'm afraid. I didn't come here to tell you what you know perfectly well when you're sane. I came here to say this: Anyone in her senses could see the game your friend here is playing. It wouldn't take a baby in. If you think that a gentleman like that [His stare travels round the dishevelled room till it rests on MALISE] champions a pretty woman for nothing, you make a fairly bad mistake.

CLARE. Take care.

But MALISE, after one convulsive movement of his hands, has again become rigid.

GEORGE. I don't pretend to be subtle or that kind of thing; but I have ordinary common sense. I don't attempt to be superior to plain facts—

CLARE. [Under her breath] Facts!

GEORGE. Oh! for goodness' sake drop that hifalutin' tone. It doesn't suit you. Look here! If you like to go abroad with one of your young sisters until the autumn, I'll let the flat and go to the Club.

CLARE. Put the fire out with a penny hose. [Slowly] I am not coming back to you, George. The farce is over.

GEORGE. [Taken aback for a moment by the finality of her tone, suddenly fronts MALISE] Then there is something between you and this fellow.

MALISE. [Dangerously, but without moving] I beg your pardon!

CLARE. There—is—nothing.

GEORGE. [Looking from one to the other] At all events, I won't, I won't see a woman who once— [CLARE makes a sudden effacing movement with her hands] I won't see her go to certain ruin without lifting a finger.

CLARE. That is noble.

GEORGE. [With intensity] I don't know that you deserve anything of me. But on my honour, as a gentleman, I came here this morning for your sake, to warn you of what you're doing. [He turns suddenly on MALISE] And I tell this precious friend of yours plainly what I think of him, and that I'm not going to play into his hands.

[MALISE, without stirring from the wall, looks at CLARE, and his lips move.]

CLARE. [Shakes her head at him—then to GEORGE] Will you go, please?

GEORGE. I will go when you do.

MALISE. A man of the world should know better than that.

GEORGE. Are you coming?

MALISE. That is inconceivable.

GEORGE. I'm not speaking to you, sir.

MALISE. You are right. Your words and mine will never kiss each other.

GEORGE. Will you come? [CLARE shakes her head]

GEORGE. [With fury] D'you mean to stay in this pigsty with that rhapsodical swine?

MALISE. [Transformed] By God, if you don't go, I'll kill you.

GEORGE. [As suddenly calm] That remains to be seen.

MALISE. [With most deadly quietness] Yes, I will kill you.

He goes stealthily along the wall, takes up from where it lies on the pile of books the great black knobby stick, and stealthily approaches GEORGE, his face quite fiendish.

CLARE. [With a swift movement, grasping the stick] Please.

MALISE resigns the stick, and the two men, perfectly still, glare at each other. CLARE, letting the stick fall, puts her foot on it. Then slowly she takes off her hat and lays it on the table.

CLARE. Now will you go! [There is silence]

GEORGE. [Staring at her hat] You mad little fool! Understand this; if you've not returned home by three o'clock I'll divorce you, and you may roll in the gutter with this high-souled friend of yours. And mind this, you sir—I won't spare you—by God! Your pocket shall suffer. That's the only thing that touches fellows like you.

Turning, he goes out, and slams the door. CLARE and MALISE remain face to face. Her lips have begun to quiver.

CLARE. Horrible!

She turns away, shuddering, and sits down on the edge of the armchair, covering her eyes with the backs of her hands. MALISE picks up the stick, and fingers it lovingly. Then putting it down, he moves so that he can see her face. She is sitting quite still, staring straight before her.

MALISE. Nothing could be better.

CLARE. I don't know what to do! I don't know what to do!

MALISE. Thank the stars for your good fortune.

CLARE. He means to have revenge on you! And it's all my fault.

MALISE. Let him. Let him go for his divorce. Get rid of him. Have done with him—somehow.

She gets up and stands with face averted. Then swiftly turning to him.

CLARE. If I must bring you harm—let me pay you back! I can't bear it otherwise! Make some use of me, if you don't mind!

MALISE. My God!

[She puts up her face to be kissed, shutting her eyes.]

MALISE. You poor—

He clasps and kisses her, then, drawing back, looks in her face. She has not moved, her eyes are still closed; but she is shivering; her lips are tightly pressed together; her hands twitching.

MALISE. [Very quietly] No, no! This is not the house of a "gentleman."

CLARE. [Letting her head fall, and almost in a whisper] I'm sorry.

MALISE. I understand.

CLARE. I don't feel. And without—I can't, can't.

MALISE. [Bitterly] Quite right. You've had enough of that.

There is a long silence. Without looking at him she takes up her hat, and puts it on.

MALISE. Not going?

[CLARE nods]

MALISE. You don't trust me?

CLARE. I do! But I can't take when I'm not giving.

MALISE. I beg—I beg you! What does it matter? Use me! Get free somehow.

CLARE. Mr. Malise, I know what I ought to be to you, if I let you in for all this. I know what you want or will want. Of course, why not?

MALISE. I give you my solemn word—

CLARE. No! if I can't be that to you—it's not real. And I can't. It isn't to be manufactured, is it?

MALISE. It is not.

CLARE. To make use of you in such a way! No.

[She moves towards the door]

MALISE. Where are you going?

CLARE does not answer. She is breathing rapidly. There is a change in her, a sort of excitement beneath her calmness.

MALISE. Not back to him? [CLARE shakes her head] Thank God! But where? To your people again?

CLARE. No.

MALISE. Nothing—desperate?

CLARE. Oh! no.

MALISE. Then what, tell me, come!

CLARE. I don't know. Women manage somehow.

MALISE. But you, poor dainty thing!

CLARE. It's all right! Don't be unhappy! Please!

MALISE. [Seizing her arm] D'you imagine they'll let you off, out there—you with your face? Come, trust me trust me! You must!

CLARE. [Holding out her hand] Good-bye!

MALISE. [Not taking that hand] This great damned world, and—you! Listen! [The sound of the traffic far down below is audible in the stillness] Into that! alone—helpless—without money. The men who work with you; the men you make friends of—d'you think they'll let you be? The men in the streets, staring at you, stopping you—pudgy, bull-necked brutes; devils with hard eyes; senile swine; and the "chivalrous" men, like me, who don't mean you harm, but can't help seeing you're made for love! Or suppose you don't take covert but struggle on in the open. Society! The respectable! The pious! Even those who love you! Will they let you be? Hue and cry! The hunt was joined the moment you broke away! It will never let up! Covert to covert—till they've run you down, and you're back in the cart, and God pity you!

CLARE. Well, I'll die running!

MALISE. No, no! Let me shelter you! Let me!

CLARE. [Shaking her head and smiling] I'm going to seek my fortune. Wish me luck!

MALISE. I can't let you go.

CLARE. You must.

He looks into her face; then, realizing that she means it, suddenly bends down to her fingers, and puts his lips to them.

MALISE. Good luck, then! Good luck!

He releases her hand. Just touching his bent head with her other hand, CLARE turns and goes. MALISE remains with bowed head, listening to the sound of her receding footsteps. They die away. He raises himself, and strikes out into the air with his clenched fist.

CURTAIN.


ACT III

MALISE'S sitting-room. An afternoon, three months later. On the table are an open bottle of claret, his hat, and some tea-things. Down in the hearth is a kettle on a lighted spirit-stand. Near the door stands HAYWOOD, a short, round-faced man, with a tobacco-coloured moustache; MALISE, by the table, is contemplating a piece of blue paper.

HAYWOOD. Sorry to press an old customer, sir, but a year and an 'alf without any return on your money—

MALISE. Your tobacco is too good, Mr. Haywood. I wish I could see my way to smoking another.

HAYWOOD. Well, sir—that's a funny remedy.

With a knock on the half-opened door, a Boy appears.

MALISE. Yes. What is it?

BOY. Your copy for "The Watchfire," please, sir.

MALISE. [Motioning him out] Yes. Wait!

The Boy withdraws. MALISE goes up to the pile of books, turns them over, and takes up some volumes.

MALISE. This is a very fine unexpurgated translation of Boccaccio's "Decameron," Mr. Haywood illustrated. I should say you would get more than the amount of your bill for them.

HAYWOOD. [Shaking his head] Them books worth three pound seven!

MALISE. It's scarce, and highly improper. Will you take them in discharge?

HAYWOOD. [Torn between emotions] Well, I 'ardly know what to say.  No, Sir, I don't think I'd like to 'ave to do with that.

MALISE. You could read them first, you know?

HAYWOOD. [Dubiously] I've got my wife at 'ome.

MALISE. You could both read them.

HAYWOOD. [Brought to his bearings] No, Sir, I couldn't.

MALISE. Very well; I'll sell them myself, and you shall have the result.

HAYWOOD. Well, thank you, sir. I'm sure I didn't want to trouble you.

MALISE. Not at all, Mr. Haywood. It's for me to apologize.

HAYWOOD. So long as I give satisfaction.

MALISE. [Holding the door for him] Certainly. Good evening.

HAYWOOD. Good evenin', sir; no offence, I hope.

MALISE. On the contrary.

Doubtfully HAYWOOD goes. And MALISE stands scratching his head; then slipping the bill into one of the volumes to remind him, he replaces them at the top of the pile. The Boy again advances into the doorway.

MALISE. Yes, now for you.

He goes to the table and takes some sheets of MS. from an old portfolio. But the door is again timidly pushed open, and HAYWOOD reappears.

MALISE. Yes, Mr. Haywood?

HAYWOOD. About that little matter, sir. If—if it's any convenience to you—I've—thought of a place where I could—

MALISE. Read them? You'll enjoy them thoroughly.

HAYWOOD. No, sir, no! Where I can dispose of them.

MALISE. [Holding out the volumes] It might be as well. [HAYWOOD takes the books gingerly] I congratulate you, Mr. Haywood; it's a classic.

HAYWOOD. Oh, indeed—yes, sir. In the event of there being any—

MALISE. Anything over? Carry it to my credit. Your bill—[He hands over the blue paper] Send me the receipt. Good evening!

HAYWOOD, nonplussed, and trying to hide the books in an evening paper, fumbles out. "Good evenin', sir!" and departs. MALISE again takes up the sheets of MS. and cons a sentence over to himself, gazing blankly at the stolid BOY.

MALISE. "Man of the world—good form your god! Poor buttoned-up philosopher" [the Boy shifts his feet] "inbred to the point of cretinism, and founded to the bone on fear of ridicule [the Boy breathes heavily]—you are the slave of facts!"

[There is a knock on the door]

MALISE. Who is it?

The door is pushed open, and REGINALD HUNTINGDON stands there.

HUNTINGDON. I apologize, sir; can I come in a minute?

[MALISE bows with ironical hostility]

HUNTINGDON. I don't know if you remember me—Clare Dedmond's brother.

MALISE. I remember you.

[He motions to the stolid Boy to go outside again]

HUNTINGDON. I've come to you, sir, as a gentleman—

MALISE. Some mistake. There is one, I believe, on the first floor.

HUNTINGDON. It's about my sister.

MALISE. Damn you! Don't you know that I've been shadowed these last three months? Ask your detectives for any information you want.

HUNTINGDON. We know that you haven't seen her, or even known where she is.

MALISE. Indeed! You've found that out? Brilliant!

HUNTINGDON. We know it from my sister.

MALISE. Oh! So you've tracked her down?

HUNTINGDON. Mrs. Fullarton came across her yesterday in one of those big shops—selling gloves.

MALISE. Mrs. Fullarton the lady with the husband. Well! you've got her. Clap her back into prison.

HUNTINGDON. We have not got her. She left at once, and we don't know where she's gone.

MALISE. Bravo!

HUNTINGDON. [Taking hold of his bit] Look here, Mr. Malise, in a way I share your feeling, but I'm fond of my sister, and it's damnable to have to go back to India knowing she must be all adrift, without protection, going through God knows what! Mrs. Fullarton says she's looking awfully pale and down.

MALISE. [Struggling between resentment and sympathy] Why do you come to me?

HUNTINGDON. We thought—

MALISE. Who?

HUNTINGDON. My, my father and myself.

MALISE. Go on.

HUNTINGDON. We thought there was just a chance that, having lost that job, she might come to you again for advice. If she does, it would be really generous of you if you'd put my father in touch with her. He's getting old, and he feels this very much. [He hands MALISE a card] This is his address.

MALISE. [Twisting the card] Let there be no mistake, sir; I do nothing that will help give her back to her husband. She's out to save her soul alive, and I don't join the hue and cry that's after her. On the contrary—if I had the power. If your father wants to shelter her, that's another matter. But she'd her own ideas about that.

HUNTINGDON. Perhaps you don't realize how unfit my sister is for rough and tumble. She's not one of this new sort of woman. She's always been looked after, and had things done for her. Pluck she's got, but that's all, and she's bound to come to grief.

MALISE. Very likely—the first birds do. But if she drops half-way it's better than if she'd never flown. Your sister, sir, is trying the wings of her spirit, out of the old slave market. For women as for men, there's more than one kind of dishonour, Captain Huntingdon, and worse things than being dead, as you may know in your profession.

HUNTINGDON. Admitted—but—

MALISE. We each have our own views as to what they are. But they all come to—death of our spirits, for the sake of our carcases. Anything more?

HUNTINGDON. My leave's up. I sail to-morrow. If you do see my sister I trust you to give her my love and say I begged she would see my father.

MALISE. If I have the chance—yes.

He makes a gesture of salute, to which HUNTINGDON responds. Then the latter turns and goes out.

MALISE. Poor fugitive! Where are you running now?

He stands at the window, through which the evening sunlight is powdering the room with smoky gold. The stolid Boy has again come in. MALISE stares at him, then goes back to the table, takes up the MS., and booms it at him; he receives the charge, breathing hard.

MALISE. "Man of the world—product of a material age; incapable of perceiving reality in motions of the spirit; having 'no use,' as you would say, for 'sentimental nonsense'; accustomed to believe yourself the national spine—your position is unassailable. You will remain the idol of the country— arbiter of law, parson in mufti, darling of the playwright and the novelist—God bless you!—while waters lap these shores."

He places the sheets of MS. in an envelope, and hands them to the Boy.

MALISE. You're going straight back to "The Watchfire"?

BOY. [Stolidly] Yes, sir.

MALISE. [Staring at him] You're a masterpiece. D'you know that?

BOY. No, sir.

MALISE. Get out, then.

He lifts the portfolio from the table, and takes it into the inner room. The Boy, putting his thumb stolidly to his nose, turns to go. In the doorway he shies violently at the figure of CLARE, standing there in a dark-coloured dress, skids past her and goes. CLARE comes into the gleam of sunlight, her white face alive with emotion or excitement. She looks round her, smiles, sighs; goes swiftly to the door, closes it, and comes back to the table. There she stands, fingering the papers on the table, smoothing MALISE's hat wistfully, eagerly, waiting.

MALISE. [Returning] You!

CLARE. [With a faint smile] Not very glorious, is it?

He goes towards her, and checks himself, then slews the armchair round.

MALISE. Come! Sit down, sit down! [CLARE, heaving a long sigh, sinks down into the chair] Tea's nearly ready.

He places a cushion for her, and prepares tea; she looks up at him softly, but as he finishes and turns to her, she drops that glance.

CLARE. Do you think me an awful coward for coming? [She has taken a little plain cigarette case from her dress] Would you mind if I smoked?

MALISE shakes his head, then draws back from her again, as if afraid to be too close. And again, unseen, she looks at him.

MALISE. So you've lost your job?

CLARE. How did you—?

MALISE. Your brother. You only just missed him. [CLARE starts up] They had an idea you'd come. He's sailing to-morrow—he wants you to see your father.

CLARE. Is father ill?

MALISE. Anxious about you.

CLARE. I've written to him every week. [Excited] They're still hunting me!

MALISE. [Touching her shoulder gently] It's all right—all right.

She sinks again into the chair, and again he withdraws. And once more she gives him that soft eager look, and once more averts it as he turns to her.

CLARE. My nerves have gone funny lately. It's being always on one's guard, and stuffy air, and feeling people look and talk about you, and dislike your being there.

MALISE. Yes; that wants pluck.

CLARE. [Shaking her head] I curl up all the time. The only thing I know for certain is, that I shall never go back to him. The more I've hated what I've been doing, the more sure I've been. I might come to anything—but not that.

MALISE. Had a very bad time?

CLARE. [Nodding] I'm spoilt. It's a curse to be a lady when you have to earn your living. It's not really been so hard, I suppose; I've been selling things, and living about twice as well as most shop girls.

MALISE. Were they decent to you?

CLARE. Lots of the girls are really nice. But somehow they don't want me, can't help thinking I've got airs or something; and in here [She touches her breast] I don't want them!

MALISE. I know.

CLARE. Mrs. Fullarton and I used to belong to a society for helping reduced gentlewomen to get work. I know now what they want: enough money not to work—that's all! [Suddenly looking up at him] Don't think me worse than I am—please! It's working under people; it's having to do it, being driven. I have tried, I've not been altogether a coward, really! But every morning getting there the same time; every day the same stale "dinner," as they call it; every evening the same "Good evening, Miss Clare," "Good evening, Miss Simpson," "Good evening, Miss Hart," "Good evening, Miss Clare." And the same walk home, or the same 'bus; and the same men that you mustn't look at, for fear they'll follow you. [She rises] Oh! and the feeling—always, always—that there's no sun, or life, or hope, or anything. It was just like being ill, the way I've wanted to ride and dance and get out into the country. [Her excitement dies away into the old clipped composure, and she sits down again] Don't think too badly of me—it really is pretty ghastly!

MALISE. [Gruffly] H'm! Why a shop?

CLARE. References. I didn't want to tell more lies than I could help; a married woman on strike can't tell the truth, you know. And I can't typewrite or do shorthand yet. And chorus—I thought—you wouldn't like.

MALISE. I? What have I—? [He checks himself] Have men been brutes?

CLARE. [Stealing a look at him] One followed me a lot. He caught hold of my arm one evening. I just took this out [She draws out her hatpin and holds it like a dagger, her lip drawn back as the lips of a dog going to bite] and said: "Will you leave me alone, please?" And he did. It was rather nice. And there was one quite decent little man in the shop—I was sorry for him—such a humble little man!

MALISE. Poor devil—it's hard not to wish for the moon.

At the tone of his voice CLARE looks up at him; his face is turned away.

CLARE. [Softly] How have you been? Working very hard?

MALISE. As hard as God will let me.

CLARE. [Stealing another look] Have you any typewriting I could do? I could learn, and I've still got a brooch I could sell. Which is the best kind?

MALISE. I had a catalogue of them somewhere.

He goes into the inner room. The moment he is gone, CLARE stands up, her hands pressed to her cheeks as if she felt them flaming. Then, with hands clasped, she stands waiting. He comes back with the old portfolio.

MALISE. Can you typewrite where you are?

CLARE. I have to find a new room anyway. I'm changing—to be safe. [She takes a luggage ticket from her glove] I took my things to Charing Cross—only a bag and one trunk. [Then, with that queer expression on her face which prefaces her desperations] You don't want me now, I suppose.

MALISE. What?

CLARE. [Hardly above a whisper] Because—if you still wanted me—I do—now.

[Etext editors note: In the 1924 revision, 11 years after this 1913 edition: "I do—now" is changed to "I could—now"— a significant change in meaning. D.W.]

MALISE. [Staring hard into her face that is quivering and smiling] You mean it? You do? You care—?

CLARE. I've thought of you so much! But only if you're sure.

He clasps her and kisses her closed eyes; and so they stand for a moment, till the sound of a latchkey in the door sends them apart.

MALISE. It's the housekeeper. Give me that ticket; I'll send for your things.

Obediently she gives him the ticket, smiles, and goes quietly into the inner room. MRS. MILER has entered; her face, more Chinese than ever, shows no sign of having seen.

MALISE. That lady will stay here, Mrs. Miler. Kindly go with this ticket to the cloak-room at Charing Cross station, and bring back her luggage in a cab. Have you money?

MRS. MILER. 'Arf a crown. [She takes the ticket—then impassively] In case you don't know—there's two o' them men about the stairs now.

The moment she is gone MALISE makes a gesture of maniacal fury. He steals on tiptoe to the outer door, and listens. Then, placing his hand on the knob, he turns it without noise, and wrenches back the door. Transfigured in the last sunlight streaming down the corridor are two men, close together, listening and consulting secretly. They start back.

MALISE. [With strange, almost noiseless ferocity] You've run her to earth; your job's done. Kennel up, hounds! [And in their faces he slams the door]

CURTAIN.


## SCENE II

SCENE II The same, early on a winter afternoon, three months later. The room has now a certain daintiness. There are curtains over the doors, a couch, under the window, all the books are arranged on shelves. In small vases, over the fireplace, are a few violets and chrysanthemums. MALISE sits huddled in his armchair drawn close to the fore, paper on knee, pen in hand. He looks rather grey and drawn, and round his chair is the usual litter. At the table, now nearer to the window, CLARE sits working a typewriter. She finishes a line, puts sheets of paper together, makes a note on a card— adds some figures, and marks the total.

CLARE. Kenneth, when this is paid, I shall have made two pound seventeen in the three months, and saved you about three pounds. One hundred and seventeen shillings at tenpence a thousand is one hundred and forty thousand words at fourteen hundred words an hour. It's only just over an hour a day. Can't you get me more?

MALISE lifts the hand that holds his pen and lets it fall again. CLARE puts the cover on the typewriter, and straps it.

CLARE. I'm quite packed. Shall I pack for you? [He nods] Can't we have more than three days at the sea? [He shakes his head. Going up to him] You did sleep last night.

MALISE. Yes, I slept.

CLARE. Bad head? [MALISE nods] By this time the day after to-morrow the case will be heard and done with. You're not worrying for me? Except for my poor old Dad, I don't care a bit.

MALISE heaves himself out of the chair, and begins pacing up and down.

CLARE. Kenneth, do you understand why he doesn't claim damages, after what he said that day-here? [Looking suddenly at him] It is true that he doesn't?

MALISE. It is not.

CLARE. But you told me yourself

MALISE. I lied.

CLARE. Why?

MALISE. [Shrugging] No use lying any longer—you'd know it tomorrow.

CLARE. How much am I valued at?

MALISE. Two thousand. [Grimly] He'll settle it on you. [He laughs] Masterly! By one stroke, destroys his enemy, avenges his "honour," and gilds his name with generosity!

CLARE. Will you have to pay?

MALISE. Stones yield no blood.

CLARE. Can't you borrow?

MALISE. I couldn't even get the costs.

CLARE. Will they make you bankrupt, then? [MALISE nods] But that doesn't mean that you won't have your income, does it? [MALISE laughs] What is your income, Kenneth? [He is silent] A hundred and fifty from "The Watchfire," I know. What else?

MALISE. Out of five books I have made the sum of forty pounds.

CLARE. What else? Tell me.

MALISE. Fifty to a hundred pounds a year. Leave me to gnaw my way out, child.

CLARE stands looking at him in distress, then goes quickly into the room behind her. MALISE takes up his paper and pen. The paper is quite blank.

MALISE. [Feeling his head] Full of smoke.

He drops paper and pen, and crossing to the room on the left goes in. CLARE re-enters with a small leather box. She puts it down on her typing table as MALISE returns followed by MRS. MILER, wearing her hat, and carrying His overcoat.

MRS. MILER. Put your coat on. It's a bitter wind.

[He puts on the coat]

CLARE. Where are you going?

MALISE. To "The Watchfire."

The door closes behind him, and MRS. MILER goes up to CLARE holding out a little blue bottle with a red label, nearly full.

MRS. MILER. You know he's takin' this [She makes a little motion towards her mouth] to make 'im sleep?

CLARE. [Reading the label] Where was it?

MRS. MILER. In the bathroom chest o' drawers, where 'e keeps 'is odds and ends. I was lookin' for 'is garters.

CLARE. Give it to me!

MRS. MILER. He took it once before. He must get his sleep.

CLARE. Give it to me!

MRS. MILER resigns it, CLARE takes the cork out, smells, then tastes it from her finger. MRS. MILER, twisting her apron in her hands, speaks.

MILS. MILER. I've 'ad it on my mind a long time to speak to yer. Your comin' 'ere's not done 'im a bit o' good.

CLARE. Don't!

MRS. MILER. I don't want to, but what with the worry o' this 'ere divorce suit, an' you bein' a lady an' 'im havin' to be so careful of yer, and tryin' to save, not smokin' all day like 'e used, an' not gettin' 'is two bottles of claret regular; an' losin' his sleep, an' takin' that stuff for it; and now this 'ere last business. I've seen 'im sometimes holdin' 'is 'ead as if it was comin' off. [Seeing CLARE wince, she goes on with a sort of compassion in her Chinese face] I can see yer fond of him; an' I've nothin' against yer you don't trouble me a bit; but I've been with 'im eight years—we're used to each other, and I can't bear to see 'im not 'imself, really I can't.

She gives a sadden sniff. Then her emotion passes, leaving her as Chinese as ever.

CLARE. This last business—what do you mean by that?

MRS. MILER. If 'e a'n't told yer, I don't know that I've any call to.

CLARE. Please.

MRS. MILER. [Her hands twisting very fast] Well, it's to do with this 'ere "Watchfire." One of the men that sees to the writin' of it 'e's an old friend of Mr. Malise, 'e come 'ere this mornin' when you was out. I was doin' my work in there [She points to the room on the right] an' the door open, so I 'earl 'em. Now you've 'ung them curtains, you can't 'elp it.

CLARE. Yes?

MRS. MILER. It's about your divorce case. This 'ere "Watchfire," ye see, belongs to some fellers that won't 'ave their men gettin' into the papers. So this 'ere friend of Mr. Malise—very nice 'e spoke about it: "If it comes into Court," 'e says, "you'll 'ave to go," 'e says. "These beggars, these dogs, these dogs," 'e says, "they'll 'oof you out," 'e says. An' I could tell by the sound of his voice, 'e meant it—proper upset 'e was. So that's that!

CLARE. It's inhuman!

MRS. MILER. That's what I thinks; but it don't 'elp, do it? "'Tain't the circulation," 'e says, "it's the principle," 'e says; and then 'e starts in swearin' horrible. 'E's a very nice man. And Mr. Malise, 'e says: "Well, that about does for me!" 'e says.

CLARE. Thank you, Mrs. Miler—I'm glad to know.

MRS. MILER. Yes; I don't know as I ought to 'ave told you. [Desperately uncomfortable] You see, I don't take notice of Mr. MALISE, but I know 'im very well. 'E's a good 'arted gentleman, very funny, that'll do things to help others, and what's more, keep on doin' 'em, when they hurt 'im; very obstinate 'e is. Now, when you first come 'ere, three months ago, I says to meself: "He'll enjoy this 'ere for a bit, but she's too much of a lady for 'im." What 'e wants about 'im permanent is a woman that thinks an' talks about all them things he talks about. And sometimes I fancy 'e don't want nothin' permanent about 'im at all.

CLARE. Don't!

MRS. MILER. [With another sudden sniff] Gawd knows I don't want to upset ye. You're situated very hard; an' women's got no business to 'urt one another—that's what I thinks.

CLARE. Will you go out and do something for me? [MRS. MILER nods]

[CLARE takes up the sheaf of papers and from the leather box a note and an emerald pendant]

Take this with the note to that address—it's quite close. He'll give you thirty pounds for it. Please pay these bills and bring me back the receipts, and what's over.

MRS. MILER. [Taking the pendant and note] It's a pretty thing.

CLARE. Yes. It was my mother's.

MRS. MILER. It's a pity to part with it; ain't you got another?

CLARE. Nothing more, Mrs. Miler, not even a wedding ring.

MRS. MILER. [Without expression] You make my 'eart ache sometimes.

[She wraps pendant and note into her handkerchief and goes out to the door.]

MRS. MILER. [From the door] There's a lady and gentleman out here. Mrs. Fuller—wants you, not Mr. Malise.

CLARE. Mrs. Fullarton? [MRS. MILER nods] Ask them to come in.

MRS. MILER opens the door wide, says "Come in," and goes. MRS. FULLARTON is accompanied not by FULLARTON, but by the lawyer, TWISDON. They come in.

MRS. FULLARTON. Clare! My dear! How are you after all this time?

CLARE. [Her eyes fixed on TWISDEN] Yes?

MRS. FULLARTON. [Disconcerted by the strange greeting] I brought Mr. Twisden to tell you something. May I stay?

CLARE. Yes. [She points to the chair at the same table: MRS. FULLARTON sits down] Now!

[TWISDEN comes forward]

TWISDEN. As you're not defending this case, Mrs. Dedmond, there is nobody but yourself for me to apply to.

CLARE. Please tell me quickly, what you've come for.

TWISDEN. [Bowing slightly] I am instructed by Mr. Dedmond to say that if you will leave your present companion and undertake not to see him again, he will withdraw the suit and settle three hundred a year on you. [At CLARE's movement of abhorrence] Don't misunderstand me, please—it is not—it could hardly be, a request that you should go back. Mr. Dedmond is not prepared to receive you again. The proposal, forgive my saying so, remarkably Quixotic, is made to save the scandal to his family and your own. It binds you to nothing but the abandonment of your present companion, with certain conditions of the same nature as to the future. In other words, it assures you a position—so long as you live quietly by yourself.

CLARE. I see. Will you please thank Mr. Dedmond, and say that I refuse?

MRS. FULLARTON. Clare, Clare! For God's sake don't be desperate.

[CLARE, deathly still, just looks at her]

TWISDEN. Mrs. Dedmond, I am bound to put the position to you in its naked brutality. You know there's a claim for damages?

CLARE. I have just learnt it.

TWISDEN. You realize what the result of this suit must be: You will be left dependent on an undischarged bankrupt. To put it another way, you'll be a stone round the neck of a drowning man.

CLARE. You are cowards.

MRS. FULLARTON. Clare, Clare! [To TWISDEN] She doesn't mean it; please be patient.

CLARE. I do mean it. You ruin him because of me. You get him down, and kick him to intimidate me.

MRS. FULLARTON. My dear girl! Mr. Twisden is not personally concerned. How can you?

CLARE. If I were dying, and it would save me, I wouldn't take a penny from my husband.

TWISDEN. Nothing could be more bitter than those words. Do you really wish me to take them back to him?

CLARE. Yes. [She turns from them to the fire]

MRS. FULLARTON. [In a low voice to TWISDEN] Please leave me alone with her, don't say anything to Mr. Dedmond yet.

TWISDEN. Mrs. Dedmond, I told you once that I wished you well. Though you have called me a coward, I still do that. For God's sake, think before it's too late.

CLARE. [Putting out her hand blindly] I'm sorry I called you a coward. It's the whole thing, I meant.

TWISDEN. Never mind that. Think!

With the curious little movement of one who sees something he does not like to see, he goes. CLARE is leaning her forehead against the mantel-shelf, seemingly unconscious that she is not alone. MRS. FULLARTON approaches quietly till she can see CLARE'S face.

MRS. FULLARTON. My dear sweet thing, don't be cross with me! [CLARE turns from her. It is all the time as if she were trying to get away from words and people to something going on within herself] How can I help wanting to see you saved from all this ghastliness?

CLARE. Please don't, Dolly! Let me be!

MRS. FULLARTON. I must speak, Clare! I do think you're hard on George. It's generous of him to offer to withdraw the suit— considering. You do owe it to us to try and spare your father and your sisters and—and all of us who care for you.

CLARE. [Facing her] You say George is generous! If he wanted to be that he'd never have claimed these damages. It's revenge he wants—I heard him here. You think I've done him an injury. So I did—when I married him. I don't know what I shall come to, Dolly, but I shan't fall so low as to take money from him. That's as certain as that I shall die.

MRS. FULLARTON. Do you know, Clare, I think it's awful about you! You're too fine, and not fine enough, to put up with things; you're too sensitive to take help, and you're not strong enough to do without it. It's simply tragic. At any rate, you might go home to your people.

CLARE. After this!

MRS. FULLARTON. To us, then?

CLARE. "If I could be the falling bee, and kiss thee all the day!" No, Dolly!

MRS. FULLARTON turns from her ashamed and baffled, but her quick eyes take in the room, trying to seize on some new point of attack.

MRS. FULLARTON. You can't be—you aren't-happy, here?

CLARE. Aren't I?

MRS. FULLARTON. Oh! Clare! Save yourself and all of us!

CLARE. [Very still] You see, I love him.

MRS. FULLARTON. You used to say you'd never love; did not want it— would never want it.

CLARE. Did I? How funny!

MRS. FULLARTON. Oh! my dear! Don't look like that, or you'll make me cry.

CLARE. One doesn't always know the future, does one? [Desperately] I love him! I love him!

MRS. FULLARTON. [Suddenly] If you love him, what will it be like for you, knowing you've ruined him?

CLARE. Go away! Go away!

MRS. FULLARTON. Love!—you said!

CLARE. [Quivering at that stab-suddenly] I must—I will keep him. He's all I've got.

MRS. FULLARTON. Can you—can you keep him?

CLARE. Go!

MRS. FULLARTON. I'm going. But, men are hard to keep, even when you've not been the ruin of them. You know whether the love this man gives you is really love. If not, God help you! [She turns at the door, and says mournfully] Good-bye, my child! If you can—

Then goes. CLARE, almost in a whisper, repeats the words: "Love! you said!" At the sound of a latchkey she runs as if to escape into the bedroom, but changes her mind and stands blotted against the curtain of the door. MALISE enters. For a moment he does not see her standing there against the curtain that is much the same colour as her dress. His face is that of a man in the grip of a rage that he feels to be impotent. Then, seeing her, he pulls himself together, walks to his armchair, and sits down there in his hat and coat.

CLARE. Well? "The Watchfire?" You may as well tell me.

MALISE. Nothing to tell you, child.

At that touch of tenderness she goes up to his chair and kneels down beside it. Mechanically MALISE takes off his hat.

CLARE. Then you are to lose that, too? [MALISE stares at her] I know about it—never mind how.

MALISE. Sanctimonious dogs!

CLARE. [Very low] There are other things to be got, aren't there?

MALISE. Thick as blackberries. I just go out and cry, "MALISE, unsuccessful author, too honest journalist, freethinker, co-respondent, bankrupt," and they tumble!

CLARE. [Quietly] Kenneth, do you care for me? [MALISE stares at her] Am I anything to you but just prettiness?

MALISE. Now, now! This isn't the time to brood! Rouse up and fight.

CLARE. Yes.

MALISE. We're not going to let them down us, are we? [She rubs her cheek against his hand, that still rests on her shoulder] Life on sufferance, breath at the pleasure of the enemy! And some day in the fullness of his mercy to be made a present of the right to eat and drink and breathe again. [His gesture sums up the rage within him] Fine! [He puts his hat on and rises] That's the last groan they get from me.

CLASS. Are you going out again? [He nods] Where?

MALISE. Blackberrying! Our train's not till six.

He goes into the bedroom. CLARE gets up and stands by the fire, looking round in a dazed way. She puts her hand up and mechanically gathers together the violets in the little vase. Suddenly she twists them to a buttonhole, and sinks down into the armchair, which he must pass. There she sits, the violets in her hand. MALISE comes out and crosses towards the outer door. She puts the violets up to him. He stares at them, shrugs his shoulders, and passes on. For just a moment CLARE sits motionless.

CLARE. [Quietly] Give me a kiss!

He turns and kisses her. But his lips, after that kiss, have the furtive bitterness one sees on the lips of those who have done what does not suit their mood. He goes out. She is left motionless by the armchair, her throat working. Then, feverishly, she goes to the little table, seizes a sheet of paper, and writes. Looking up suddenly she sees that MRS. MILER has let herself in with her latchkey.

MRS. MILER. I've settled the baker, the milk, the washin' an' the groceries—this 'ere's what's left.

She counts down a five-pound note, four sovereigns, and two shillings on to the little table. CLARE folds the letter into an envelope, then takes up the five-pound note and puts it into her dress.

CLARE. [Pointing to the money on the table] Take your wages; and give him this when he comes in. I'm going away.

MRS. MILER. Without him? When'll you be comin' back?

CLARE. [Rising] I shan't be coming back. [Gazing at MRS. MILER'S hands, which are plaiting at her dress] I'm leaving Mr. Malise, and shan't see him again. And the suit against us will be withdrawn—the divorce suit—you understand?

MRS. MILER. [Her face all broken up] I never meant to say anything to yer.

CLARE. It's not you. I can see for myself. Don't make it harder; help me. Get a cab.

MRS. MILER. [Disturbed to the heart] The porter's outside, cleanin' the landin' winder.

CLARE. Tell him to come for my trunk. It is packed. [She goes into the bedroom]

MRS. MILER. [Opening the door-desolately] Come 'ere!

[The PORTER appears in shirt-sleeves at the door]

MRS. MILER. The lady wants a cab. Wait and carry 'er trunk down.

CLARE comes from the bedroom in her hat and coat.

MRS. MILER. [TO the PORTER] Now.

They go into the bedroom to get the trunk. CLARE picks up from the floor the bunch of violets, her fingers play with it as if they did not quite know what it was; and she stands by the armchair very still, while MRS. MILER and the PORTER pass her with trunk and bag. And even after the PORTER has shouldered the trunk outside, and marched away, and MRS. MILER has come back into the room, CLARE still stands there.

MRS. MILER. [Pointing to the typewriter] D'you want this 'ere, too?

CLARE. Yes.

MRS. MILER carries it out. Then, from the doorway, gazing at CLARE taking her last look, she sobs, suddenly. At sound of that sob CLARE throws up her head.

CLARE. Don't! It's all right. Good-bye!

She walks out and away, not looking back. MRS. MILER chokes her sobbing into the black stuff of her thick old jacket.

CURTAIN

## ACT IV

Supper-time in a small room at "The Gascony" on Derby Day. Through the windows of a broad corridor, out of which the door opens, is seen the dark blue of a summer night. The walls are of apricot-gold; the carpets, curtains, lamp-shades, and gilded chairs, of red; the wood-work and screens white; the palms in gilded tubs. A doorway that has no door leads to another small room. One little table behind a screen, and one little table in the open, are set for two persons each. On a service-table, above which hangs a speaking-tube, are some dishes of hors d'ouvres, a basket of peaches, two bottles of champagne in ice-pails, and a small barrel of oysters in a gilded tub. ARNAUD, the waiter, slim, dark, quick, his face seamed with a quiet, soft irony, is opening oysters and listening to the robust joy of a distant supper-party, where a man is playing the last bars of: "Do ye ken John Peel" on a horn. As the sound dies away, he murmurs: "Tres Joli!" and opens another oyster. Two Ladies with bare shoulders and large hats pass down the corridor. Their talk is faintly wafted in: "Well, I never like Derby night! The boys do get so bobbish!" "That horn—vulgar, I call it!" ARNAUD'S eyebrows rise, the corners of his mouth droop. A Lady with bare shoulders, and crimson roses in her hair, comes along the corridor, and stops for a second at the window, for a man to join her. They come through into the room. ARNAUD has sprung to attention, but with: "Let's go in here, shall we?" they pass through into the further room. The MANAGER, a gentleman with neat moustaches, and buttoned into a frock-coat, has appeared, brisk, noiseless, his eyes everywhere; he inspects the peaches.

MANAGER. Four shillin' apiece to-night, see?

ARNAUD. Yes, Sare.

From the inner room a young man and his partner have come in. She is dark, almost Spanish-looking; he fair, languid, pale, clean-shaved, slackly smiling, with half-closed eyes-one of those who are bred and dissipated to the point of having lost all save the capacity for hiding their emotions. He speaks in a—

LANGUID VOICE. Awful row they're kickin' up in there, Mr. Varley. A fellow with a horn.

MANAGER. [Blandly] Gaddesdon Hunt, my lord—always have their supper with us, Derby night. Quiet corner here, my lord. Arnaud!

ARNAUD is already at the table, between screen and palm. And, there ensconced, the couple take their seats. Seeing them safely landed, the MANAGER, brisk and noiseless, moves away. In the corridor a lady in black, with a cloak falling open, seems uncertain whether to come in. She advances into the doorway. It is CLARE.

ARNAUD. [Pointing to the other table as he flies with dishes] Nice table, Madame.

CLARE moves to the corner of it. An artist in observation of his clients, ARNAUD takes in her face— very pale under her wavy, simply-dressed hair; shadowy beneath the eyes; not powdered; her lips not reddened; without a single ornament; takes in her black dress, finely cut, her arms and neck beautifully white, and at her breast three gardenias. And as he nears her, she lifts her eyes. It is very much the look of something lost, appealing for guidance.

ARNAUD. Madame is waiting for someone? [She shakes her head] Then Madame will be veree well here—veree well. I take Madame's cloak?

He takes the cloak gently and lays it on the back of the chair fronting the room, that she may put it round her when she wishes. She sits down.

LANGUID VOICE. [From the corner] Waiter!

ARNAUD. Milord!

LANGUID VOICE. The Roederer.

ARNAUD. At once, Milord.

CLARE sits tracing a pattern with her finger on the cloth, her eyes lowered. Once she raises them, and follows ARNAUD's dark rapid figure.

ARNAUD. [Returning] Madame feels the 'eat? [He scans her with increased curiosity] You wish something, Madame?

CLARE. [Again giving him that look] Must I order?

ARNAUD. Non, Madame, it is not necessary. A glass of water. [He pours it out] I have not the pleasure of knowing Madame's face.

CLARE. [Faintly smiling] No.

ARNAUD. Madame will find it veree good 'ere, veree quiet.

LANGUID VOICE. Waiter!

ARNAUD. Pardon! [He goes]

The bare-necked ladies with large hats again pass down the corridor outside, and again their voices are wafted in: "Tottie! Not she! Oh! my goodness, she has got a pride on her!" "Bobbie'll never stick it!" "Look here, dear—" Galvanized by those sounds, CLARE has caught her cloak and half-risen; they die away and she subsides.

ARNAUD. [Back at her table, with a quaint shrug towards the corridor] It is not rowdy here, Madame, as a rule—not as in some places. To-night a little noise. Madame is fond of flowers? [He whisks out, and returns almost at once with a bowl of carnations from some table in the next room] These smell good!

CLARE. You are very kind.

ARNAUD. [With courtesy] Not at all, Madame; a pleasure. [He bows]

A young man, tall, thin, hard, straight, with close-cropped, sandyish hair and moustache, a face tanned very red, and one of those small, long, lean heads that only grow in Britain; clad in a thin dark overcoat thrown open, an opera hat pushed back, a white waistcoat round his lean middle, he comes in from the corridor. He looks round, glances at CLARE, passes her table towards the further room, stops in the doorway, and looks back at her. Her eyes have just been lifted, and are at once cast down again. The young man wavers, catches ARNAUD's eye, jerks his head to summon him, and passes into the further room. ARNAUD takes up the vase that has been superseded, and follows him out. And CLARE sits alone in silence, broken by the murmurs of the languid lord and his partner, behind the screen. She is breathing as if she had been running hard. She lifts her eyes. The tall young man, divested of hat and coat, is standing by her table, holding out his hand with a sort of bashful hardiness.

YOUNG MAN. How d'you do? Didn't recognize you at first. So sorry —awfully rude of me.

CLARE'S eyes seem to fly from him, to appeal to him, to resign herself all at once. Something in the YOUNG MAN responds. He drops his hand.

CLARE. [Faintly] How d'you do?

YOUNG MAN. [Stammering] You, you been down there to-day?

CLARE. Where?

YOUNG MAN. [With a smile] The Derby. What? Don't you generally go down? [He touches the other chair] May I?

CLARE. [Almost in a whisper] Yes.

As he sits down, ARNAUD returns and stands before them.

ARNAUD. The plovers' eggs veree good to-night, Sare. Veree good, Madame. A peach or two, after. Veree good peaches. The Roederer, Sare—not bad at all. Madame likes it frappe, but not too cold— yes?

[He is away again to his service-table.]

YOUNG MAN. [Burying his face in the carnations] I say—these are jolly, aren't they? They do you pretty well here.

CLARE. Do they?

YOUNG MAN. You've never been here? [CLARE shakes her head] By Jove! I thought I didn't know your face. [CLARE looks full at him. Again something moves in the YOUNG MAN, and he stammers] I mean—not—

CLARE. It doesn't matter.

YOUNG MAN. [Respectfully] Of course, if I—if you were waiting for anybody, or anything—I——

[He half rises]

CLARE. It's all right, thank you.

The YOUNG MAN sits down again, uncomfortable, nonplussed. There is silence, broken by the inaudible words of the languid lord, and the distant merriment of the supper-party. ARNAUD brings the plovers' eggs.

YOUNG MAN. The wine, quick.

ARNAUD. At once, Sare.

YOUNG MAN. [Abruptly] Don't you ever go racing, then?

CLARE. No.

[ARNAUD pours out champagne]

YOUNG MAN. I remember awfully well my first day. It was pretty thick, lost every blessed bob, and my watch and chain, playin' three cards on the way home.

CLARE. Everything has a beginning, hasn't it?

[She drinks. The YOUNG MAN stares at her]

YOUNG MAN. [Floundering in these waters deeper than he had bargained for] I say—about things having beginnings—did you mean anything?

[CLARE nods]

YOUNG MAN. What! D'you mean it's really the first—?

CLARE nods. The champagne has flicked her courage.

YOUNG MAN. By George! [He leans back] I've often wondered.

ARNAUD. [Again filling the glasses] Monsieur finds—

YOUNG MAN. [Abruptly] It's all right.

He drains his glass, then sits bolt upright. Chivalry and the camaraderie of class have begun to stir in him.

YOUNG MAN. Of course I can see that you're not—I mean, that you're a—a lady. [CLARE smiles] And I say, you know—if you have to— because you're in a hole—I should feel a cad. Let me lend you—?

CLARE. [Holding up her glass] 'Le vin est tiré, il faut le boire'!

She drinks. The French words, which he does not too well understand, completing his conviction that she is a lady, he remains quite silent, frowning. As CLARE held up her glass, two gentlemen have entered. The first is blond, of good height and a comely insolence. His crisp, fair hair, and fair brushed-up moustache are just going grey; an eyeglass is fixed in one of two eyes that lord it over every woman they see; his face is broad, and coloured with air and wine. His companion is a tall, thin, dark bird of the night, with sly, roving eyes, and hollow cheeks. They stand looking round, then pass into the further room; but in passing, they have stared unreservedly at CLARE.

YOUNG MAN. [Seeing her wince] Look here! I'm afraid you must feel me rather a brute, you know.

CLARE. No, I don't; really.

YOUNG MAN. Are you absolute stoney? [CLARE nods] But [Looking at her frock and cloak] you're so awfully well—

CLARE. I had the sense to keep them.

YOUNG MAN. [More and more disturbed] I say, you know—I wish you'd let me lend you something. I had quite a good day down there.

CLARE. [Again tracing her pattern on the cloth—then looking up at him full] I can't take, for nothing.

YOUNG MAN. By Jove! I don't know-really, I don't—this makes me feel pretty rotten. I mean, it's your being a lady.

CLARE. [Smiling] That's not your fault, is it? You see, I've been beaten all along the line. And I really don't care what happens to me. [She has that peculiar fey look on her face now] I really don't; except that I don't take charity. It's lucky for me it's you, and not some—

The supper-party is getting still more boisterous, and there comes a long view holloa, and a blast of the horn.

YOUNG MAN. But I say, what about your people? You must have people of some sort.

He is fast becoming fascinated, for her cheeks have begun to flush and her eyes to shine.

CLARE. Oh, yes; I've had people, and a husband, and—everything— And here I am! Queer, isn't it? [She touches her glass] This is going to my head! Do you mind? I sha'n't sing songs and get up and dance, and I won't cry, I promise you!

YOUNG MAN. [Between fascination and chivalry] By George! One simply can't believe in this happening to a lady.

CLARE. Have you got sisters? [Breaking into her soft laughter] My brother's in India. I sha'n't meet him, anyway.

YOUNG MAN. No, but—I say-are you really quite cut off from everybody? [CLARE nods] Something rather awful must have happened?

She smiles. The two gentlemen have returned. The blond one is again staring fixedly at CLARE. This time she looks back at him, flaming; and, with a little laugh, he passes with his friend into the corridor.

CLARE. Who are those two?

YOUNG MAN. Don't know—not been much about town yet. I'm just back from India myself. You said your brother was there; what's his regiment?

CLARE. [Shaking her head] You're not going to find out my name. I haven't got one—nothing.

She leans her bare elbows on the table, and her face on her hands.

CLARE. First of June! This day last year I broke covert—I've been running ever since.

YOUNG MAN. I don't understand a bit. You—must have had a—a—some one—

But there is such a change in her face, such rigidity of her whole body, that he stops and averts his eyes. When he looks again she is drinking. She puts the glass down, and gives a little laugh.

YOUNG MAN. [With a sort of awe] Anyway it must have been like riding at a pretty stiff fence, for you to come here to-night.

CLARE. Yes. What's the other side?

The YOUNG MAN puts out his hand and touches her arm. It is meant for sympathy, but she takes it for attraction.

CLARE. [Shaking her head] Not yet please! I'm enjoying this. May I have a cigarette?

[He takes out his case, and gives her one]

CLARE. [Letting the smoke slowly forth] Yes, I'm enjoying it. Had a pretty poor time lately; not enough to eat, sometimes.

YOUNG MAN. Not really! How damnable! I say, do have something more substantial.

CLARE gives a sudden gasp, as if going off into hysterical laughter, but she stifles it, and shakes her head.

YOUNG MAN. A peach?

[ARNAUD brings peaches to the table]

CLARE. [Smiling] Thank you.

[He fills their glasses and retreats]

CLARE. [Raising her glass] Eat and drink, for tomorrow we—Listen!

From the supper-party comes the sound of an abortive chorus: "With a hey ho, chivy, hark forrard, hark forrard, tantivy!" Jarring out into a discordant whoop, it sinks.

CLARE. "This day a stag must die." Jolly old song!

YOUNG MAN. Rowdy lot! [Suddenly] I say—I admire your pluck.

CLARE. [Shaking her head] Haven't kept my end up. Lots of women do! You see: I'm too fine, and not fine enough! My best friend said that. Too fine, and not fine enough. [She laughs] I couldn't be a saint and martyr, and I wouldn't be a soulless doll. Neither one thing nor the other—that's the tragedy.

YOUNG MAN. You must have had awful luck!

CLARE. I did try. [Fiercely] But what's the good—when there's nothing before you?—Do I look ill?

YOUNG MAN. No; simply awfully pretty.

CLARE. [With a laugh] A man once said to me: "As you haven't money, you should never have been pretty!" But, you see, it is some good. If I hadn't been, I couldn't have risked coming here, could I? Don't you think it was rather sporting of me to buy these [She touches the gardenias] with the last shilling over from my cab fare?

YOUNG MAN. Did you really? Damned sporting!

CLARE. It's no use doing things by halves, is it? I'm in for it— wish me luck! [She drinks, and puts her glass down with a smile] In for it—deep! [She flings up her hands above her smiling face] Down, down, till they're just above water, and then—down, down, down, and—all over! Are you sorry now you came and spoke to me?

YOUNG MAN. By Jove, no! It may be caddish, but I'm not.

CLARE. Thank God for beauty! I hope I shall die pretty! Do you think I shall do well?

YOUNG MAN. I say, don't talk like that!

CLARE. I want to know. Do you?

YOUNG MAN. Well, then—yes, I do.

CLARE. That's splendid. Those poor women in the streets would give their eyes, wouldn't they?— that have to go up and down, up and down! Do you think I—shall—

The YOUNG MAN, half-rising, puts his hand on her arm.

YOUNG MAN. I think you're getting much too excited. You look all— Won't you eat your peach? [She shakes her head] Do! Have something else, then—some grapes, or something?

CLARE. No, thanks.

[She has become quite calm again]

YOUNG MAN. Well, then, what d'you think? It's awfully hot in here, isn't it? Wouldn't it be jollier drivin'? Shall we—shall we make a move?

CLARE. Yes.

The YOUNG MAN turns to look for the waiter, but ARNAUD is not in the room. He gets up.

YOUNG MAN. [Feverishly] Damn that waiter! Wait half a minute, if you don't mind, while I pay the bill.

As he goes out into the corridor, the two gentlemen re-appear. CLARE is sitting motionless, looking straight before her.

DARK ONE. A fiver you don't get her to!

BLOND ONE. Done!

He advances to her table with his inimitable insolence, and taking the cigar from his mouth, bends his stare on her, and says: "Charmed to see you lookin' so well! Will you have supper with me here to-morrow night?" Startled out of her reverie, CLARE looks up. She sees those eyes, she sees beyond him the eyes of his companion-sly, malevolent, amused-watching; and she just sits gazing, without a word. At that regard, so clear, the BLOND ONE does not wince. But rather suddenly he says: "That's arranged then. Half-past eleven. So good of you. Good-night!" He replaces his cigar and strolls back to his companion, and in a low voice says: "Pay up!" Then at a languid "Hullo, Charles!" they turn to greet the two in their nook behind the screen. CLARE has not moved, nor changed the direction of her gaze. Suddenly she thrusts her hand into the, pocket of the cloak that hangs behind her, and brings out the little blue bottle which, six months ago, she took from MALISE. She pulls out the cork and pours the whole contents into her champagne. She lifts the glass, holds it before her—smiling, as if to call a toast, then puts it to her lips and drinks. Still smiling, she sets the empty glass down, and lays the gardenia flowers against her face. Slowly she droops back in her chair, the drowsy smile still on her lips; the gardenias drop into her lap; her arms relax, her head falls forward on her breast. And the voices behind the screen talk on, and the sounds of joy from the supper-party wax and wane. The waiter, ARNAUD, returning from the corridor, passes to his service-table with a tall, beribboned basket of fruit. Putting it down, he goes towards the table behind the screen, and sees. He runs up to CLARE.

ARNAUD. Madame! Madame! [He listens for her breathing; then suddenly catching sight of the little bottle, smells at it] Bon Dieu!

[At that queer sound they come from behind the screen—all four, and look. The dark night bird says: "Hallo; fainted!" ARNAUD holds out the bottle.]

LANGUID LORD. [Taking it, and smelling] Good God! [The woman bends over CLARE, and lifts her hands; ARNAUD rushes to his service-table, and speaks into his tube]

ARNAUD. The boss. Quick! [Looking up he sees the YOUNG MAN, returning] 'Monsieur, elle a fui! Elle est morte'!

LANGUID LORD. [To the YOUNG MAN standing there aghast] What's this? Friend of yours?

YOUNG MAN. My God! She was a lady. That's all I know about her.

LANGUID LORD. A lady!

[The blond and dark gentlemen have slipped from the room; and out of the supper-party's distant laughter comes suddenly a long, shrill: "Gone away!" And the sound of the horn playing the seven last notes of the old song: "This day a stag must die!" From the last note of all the sound flies up to an octave higher, sweet and thin, like a spirit passing, till it is drowned once more in laughter. The

YOUNG MAN has covered his eyes with his hands; ARNAUD is crossing himself fervently; the LANGUID LORD stands gazing, with one of the dropped gardenias twisted in his fingers; and the woman, bending over CLARE, kisses her forehead.]

CURTAIN.


## JOHN GALSWORTHY – A SHORT BIOGRAPHY

John Galsworthy, eldest son of John Galsworthy (1817-1904), a solicitor and company director of Old Jewry, London, and Blanche Bailey (1835-1915), daughter of Charles Bartleet, a needlemaker in Redditch. His father's ancestors originated in Wembury, near Plymouth in England, and Galsworthy, for whom family origins were of significant importance, maintained a close connection with Devon. His more immediate family were considerably wealthy and well established in the shipping industry, and owned a fine estate in Kingston-upon-Thames called Parkfield, where Galsworthy was born on the 14th August 1867. At the age of nine he began education at Saugeen, a Bournemouth preparatory school, before starting at Harrow school in 1881 where he remained until 1886, distinguishing himself as an athlete.

His education at Harrow being successful enough to gain him entrance to Oxford, he began at New College to read law and gained a second-class degree with honours in 1889. Following Lincoln's Inn he was called to the bar in 1890. Despite this recognition he realised that he was not keen to actually begin practising law and so he resolved instead to look after the family's shipping business while specialising himself in Marine Law. This decision saw him take to the seas to destinations such as Vancouver, Island and South AFrica, though it was at the age of twenty-five on one particular journey to Australia, motivated by an (unfulfilled) intention to meet Robert Louis Stevenson on Samoa that he would being to realise fully his literary interests: though he was not considering becoming a writer at this time, his enjoyment of literature was enough to encourage an attempt at meeting a great writer and eventually enabled one of the most significant encounters of his life. He made the journey with his friend Edward Sanderson and, though he missed Stevenson, he met Joseph Conrad, a fellow future author famed for his novels which were often nautically themed. At the time Conrad was the first mate of the sailing-ship Torrens moored in the harbour of Adelaide, Australia; still very much focused on his ship-borne career, he was yet to begin his writing in earnest.

Indeed, though neither knew at the time, both Conrad and Galsworthy were at similar junctures in their lives, their time spent as sea acting as a transitional period during which each found their literary calling. It is perhaps owning to this unknown common ground that they became close friends. During his time on the Torrens Galsworthy recorded several details, offering a frank and valuable characterisation of Conrad while also illuminating his own experiences as a student of Marine Law.

"I supposed to be studying navigation for the Admiralty Bar, would every day work out the position of the ship with the captain. On one side of the saloon table we would sit and check our observations with those of Conrad, who from the other side of the table would look at us a little quizzically."

On his return to England and the cessation of his nautical voyaging, Galsworthy began an affair with the wife of his first cousin, Major Arthur John Galsworthy. Ada Nemesis Pearson Cooper (1864-1956), the daughter of Emanuel Copper, an obstetrician from Norwich, remained married to the Major for ten years and the affair remained secret for its duration. In order to conceal the affair they took considerable pains to avoid suspicion. One such tactic was to stay in a secluded farmhouse called Wingstone in the village on Manaton on Dartmoor, in Devon. In Galsworthy's decision to choose Devon as the location for their clandestine rendezvous we see evidence of Galsworthy's affection for the place of his father's origin. It was only when, in 1905, she divorced the Major that their affair became known following their marriage on 23rd September of that year.

Galsworthy now took to writing sometime after having met Conrad and his career began in earnest when, in 1897, his first work, From the Four Winds, a volume of short stories, was published under the pseudonym John Sinjohn. He succeeded this in 1898 with Jocelyn, his first novel, and then his second in 1900, Villa Rubein. In 1901 he published a second volume of short stories, A Man of Devon, which was the last of his work to be published under pseudonym. The first of his work to be published under his own name was The Island Pharisees in 1904, a novel of social observation, seasoned with flashes of satire and propaganda. His decision to write under his own name is arguably owing to the recent death of his father, either as a mark of respect to his name or because now he was able to publish freely without incurring the possibility of paternal disappointment at his choice of career. It also marked a shift in his professionalism; he had hitherto published with small, independent publishers, but The Island Pharisees was published by Heinemann, a far more established House and one with whom he remained for the duration of his writing career.

He arguably cemented his position and maturity as a writer when, in 1906, he saw the publication of both his first major play, The Silver Box, and the novel The Man of Property. Each was published to considerable critical acclaim, and to achieve both in such a short space of time was impressive. the Silver Box concerns the imbalance in the justice system with regards to criminals of differing class by contrasting the treatment of a poor thief and a rich thief, both of whom stole silver cigarette cases but for very different reasons. The complexity of individual experience when not dealt with in public is highlighted and questioned in a bravely critical manner; despite the clear issues it raises with class and privilege, the final night was attended by the Price and Princess of Wales. The Man of Property was the first novel in the famous The Forsyte Saga, a trilogy of novels with an 'interlude' between each one, written between 1906 and 1921. Dealing with the questions of status, class and materialism, The Man of Property introduces us to the Forsyte family, particularly Soames Forsyte, who is acutely aware of his status as 'new money' and equally keen to assert himself as a wealthy man. Jealous of his wife and desperate to own things in order to confirm his wealth to those observing him, he engineers a plan to keep his wife from her friends which backfires spectacularly when, instead of cutting her off, all Soames achieves is enabling her to have an affair. This drives Soames to terrible actions with terrible consequences, which Galsworthy depicts with confidence.

Very typically Edwardian, the novel focuses on conflict between property and art, and to a certain degree much of its emotional power is drawn from Galsworthy's own life, particularly his affair with Ada. Their rendezvous in the countryside of Devon mirror the manner in which Forsyte seeks to relocate his wife and; though theirs was a much healthier relationship, there are clear similarities. By examining the fragile nature of the class system and those moving within it Galsworthy offered an important perspective on the relationships between material wealth, personal happiness and obsession, and the manner in which these change over time. His contemporaries widely regarded the publication of this novel as marking the end of Victorianism. His friend Conrad praised it as "indubitably a piece of art" and, though the notoriously risqué D.H. Lawrence lamented the novel's timidity in the face of sexuality and sensuality, he considered it potentially "a very great novel, a very great satire".

Though he continued to write both plays and novels, it was his work as a playwright for which he was most celebrated by his contemporaries. Indeed, his next novel, The Country House, seems uncharacteristically unfocused, its satirical view of those belonging to the country set comparatively unremarkable and weakly characterised, while at times the tone of satire becomes one of ironic detachment. In 1909 he published Fraternity, an exploration of of the various connections between urban society and the social classes therein, though its representation of lower-class Londoners is utterly unconvincing and ill-informed. Remaining with the subject of the landed gentry and the society surrounding it, in 1915 he published The Freelands, which does not stray far from conservative discussions of capitalism, the rural economy and their interrelationship.

His drama, however, featured a convincingly muted realism, directed at a relatively small, educated and politically-aware audience. His social agenda is prevalent here too, and is represented in a simple and static manner producing arresting instances of high drama. This talent for creating moments of captivating theatre is complimented by an instinctual sense of balance enabling his narratives to vacillate between their emotional high- and low-points, ultimately reaching conclusive equilibrium. This is particularly evident in one of his most popular plays, Strife, published in 1909 and examining the antagonists in a strike at a Cornish tin mine. In this, and in 1910's Justice, he approaches his subject with sympathy, irony and balance, which establishes a position of narrative authority while garnering the audiences trust that he is representing his characters and their motives justly. Justice condemns the use of solitary confinement in prisons, a reformist agenda which caught the liberality of his contemporary audiences along with the home secretary, Winston Churchill. Despite he was careful to disassociate himself with politics and professed himself apolitical, he and his work were nevertheless aligned with the views of the Liberal establishment. He spent much of the duration of the First World War working in a field hospital in France as an orderly having been passed over for military service.

Despite the popularity and brilliance of his work, it was only in 1920 that he had his first true commercial success with The Skin Game, a melodrama dealing with ethics, property and class. The play was adapted by Alfred Hitchcock in 1931. Galsworthy, meanwhile, had turned down a knighthood in 1918, considering his work not sufficient to be made a knight of the realm. He did, however, accept the Belgian Palmes d'Or in the following year. In 1920 he published the second novel in the Forsyte Saga, In Chancery, in which he resumes many of the themes of the first novel, focusing on the marital disharmony between Soames Forsyte and his wife. Katherine Mansfield considered it "a fascinating, brilliant book" in her review in The Atheneum. Then, in 1921, he was elected as the PEN International Literary Club's first president. The concluding novel to The Forsyte Saga, To Let was published in 1921 with a kind of peace being found between Forsyte and his now-ex wife, though he is left contemplating his losses and his greed. More ironic treatment of class confusions followed in Loyalties, bringing with it more popular success which lasted until 1926 and Escape, the last of his popular plays. Though he enjoyed popular success it was inconsistent and relatively small. His Collected Plays was published in 1929.

Over the course of time the appreciation of his work has gradually shifted from his plays to his novels, and particularly the detail and intricacy of his chronicle of English social difference, tension and pretension in The Forsyte Saga. Its success encouraged Galsworthy to revisit Soames Forsyte in a second trilogy, A Modern Comedy, which follows Soames's obsessive love of his daughter Fleur. In its three volumes, The White Monkey (1924), The Silver Spoon (1936) and Swan Song (1928) he examines the English commercial upper-middle class and its ideologies, its instinct to possess as its only way of distinguishing itself manifested in the poisonous materialism of Soames. Interestingly, this emergent social class which he so vehemently criticises is the very class from which he emerged. He witnessed first-hand its insularity, its chauvinism, its restrictive and oppressive morality, its stubborn imperialism and its materialism, and it is this experience which enables him to write so comfortably about it. Swan Song is widely considered among the best of Galsworthy's writing for the depth of its exploration of society and its heightened emotional subtlety. In 1929 he was appointed to the Order of Merit, despite having turned down a knighthood earlier. He spent his last years writing a third trilogy, End of the Chapter, beginning in 1931 with Maid in Waiting, Flowering

Wilderness in 1932 and concluding with Over The River in 1933. These are significantly less coherent works and are indicative of his deteriorating health. Indeed, in 1932 he was awarded the Nobel Prize, though he was too ill to attend the ceremony.

Throughout the course of his career he received honorary degrees from the universities of St Andrews (1922), Manchester (1927), Dublin (1929), Cambridge (1930), Sheffield (1930), Oxford (1931), and Princeton (1931). In 1926 New College, Oxford, elected him as an honorary fellow. In photographs he is portrayed as handsome, fastidiously dressed and dignified. He was unusually compassionate and this saw him involved in several charitable and humane causes throughout the course of his life, including penal reforms, attacks on theatrical censorship and campaigning for animal rights. Though he spent the majority of the final seven years of his life at his home in Bury, West Sussex, it was at his home in Hampstead, London, that he died of a brain tumour on 31st January, 1933, six weeks after having been too ill to attend the ceremony in honour of his receiving the Nobel Prize. According to demands made in his will he was cremated and his ashes scattered over the South Downs from an aeroplane. Also in his will was his wish to leave cottages to several of his astonished tenants. He is memorialised in Highgate 'New' Cemetery and in the cloisters of New College, Oxford, where he was an honorary fellow.

www.ingramcontent.com/pod-product-compliance
Lightning Source LLC
Chambersburg PA
CBHW061457170626
46811CB00004B/1557